J. T. EDSON'S
FLOATING OUTFIT

The toughest bunch of Rebels that ever lost a war, they fought for the South, and then for Texas, as the legendary Floating Outfit of "Ole Devil" Hardin's O.D. Connected ranch.

MARK COUNTER was the best-dressed man in the West: always dressed fit-to-kill. **BELLE BOYD** was as deadly as she was beautiful, with a "Manhattan" model Colt tucked under her long skirts. **THE YSABEL KID** was Comanche fast and Texas tough. And the most famous of them all was **DUSTY FOG**, the ex-cavalryman known as the Rio Hondo Gun Wizard.

J. T. Edson has captured all the excitement and adventure of the raw frontier in this magnificent Western series. Turn the page for a complete list of Berkley Floating Outfit titles.

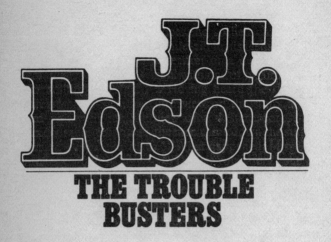

J.T. Edson

THE TROUBLE BUSTERS

BERKLEY BOOKS, NEW YORK

Originally published in Great Britain by Brown Watson Ltd.

This Berkley book contains the complete
text of the original edition.
It has been completely reset in a type face
designed for easy reading, and was printed
from new film.

THE TROUBLE BUSTERS

A Berkley Book / published by arrangement with
Transworld Publishers, Ltd.

PRINTING HISTORY
Brown Watson edition published 1965
Corgi edition published 1969
Berkley edition / February 1982

ISBN: 0-425-05227-3

A BERKLEY BOOK ® TM 757,375
Berkley Books are published by Berkley Publishing Corporation,
200 Madison Avenue, New York, New York 10016.
PRINTED IN THE UNITED STATES OF AMERICA

AUTHOR'S NOTE

*While complete in itself, the events in this book
run concurrently with those told in
THE MAKING OF A LAWMAN*

CHAPTER ONE

Crisis in Mulrooney

"I tell you, Miss Freddie, I saw a drive headed for Brownton this morning."

The speaker leaned both hands on the polished top of the table as he spoke, looking across it at Freddie Woods who sat in the place of honor. Then he stiffened up again for he had no wish to show disrespect to the woman.

None of the men at the table wished to show anything but respect to Freddie. Most of them owed her something; all owed their presence in the town of Mulrooney, Kansas, to her persuasion and lead. It had been Freddie who stirred them up in their dying town back East, gave them the idea of moving out West and provided the incentive for them to make the journey to where they could found a town along the ever-advancing railroad, in the hope of waxing rich from the Texas trail drive trade.

And why not?

The herds from Texas must come to the railroad to find a market. There did not appear to be any reason why the trail bosses should not select Mulrooney as the point where they met the cattle-buyers from the East.

What then caused the concern among the members of the town council as they sat around a table in the comfortable, well-furnished dining room of Freddie's suite on the floor above her Fair Lady Saloon?

1

One thing. A small thing the Kansas City Land Office agent forgot to mention. Nothing much really; the kind of thing a man with his eye on a large commission as a result of so extensive a sale of land might be excused for overlooking.

There was a second town with exactly the same aims in mind not six miles west along the railroad track.

By the time the citizens of Mulrooney learned this detail, they had invested their savings in building stock-pens, homes, business premises of various kinds, a stout stone jail – which ought to pay for itself in fines levied against various law-breaking visitors – a strongly made, well-equipped bank where the cattle-buyers could leave their wealth in safety, and all the other amenities a trail-end town would need.

Brownton, the rival town, had much the same amenities and was built, as Mulrooney had been, ready for the start of another year's trail drive season. Then both towns sat back and waited for the long-horned wealth of the Lone Star State to walk north into their hands. Both towns might survive, but that was doubtful. They were too close together and one would almost certainly receive the bulk of the trade while the other gradually starved out.

Now it seemed that the first drive of the year had gone into Brownton. The news brought the town council to Freddie's rooms to convene a meeting and discuss ways and means of saving their investments.

"The others will follow," Shadrack Birnbaum pointed out, nervously twisting a whisky glass between fat fingers.

"Not necessarily," objected Cyrus Coutland, the big, burly and shrewd town banker. "From what I heard it was only a small local herd."

Birnbaum shook his head. He was a small, fat, merry-looking man with an amazing capacity for worry. The only time Birnbaum seemed content was when he had a pile of worries gathered over his head.

"But the hands from that herd will go down trail and tell others about Brownton," he said. "I don't know much about cattle drives, but I can't see a trail boss going looking for a town that might exist when he hears about another town that certainly exists. That's logic."

"As you say, Shad," Freddie Woods answered. "That's logic."

Turning her grave face from Birnbaum, Freddie looked at the other men around the table. Coutland everlastingly chewing on his cigar; Schafer the hotel keeper drumming his fingers on the table top; Sherill, who with Birnbaum represented the storekeepers' interests; Dongelon, owner of the only other saloon so far open, and Sanders, the railroad depot agent. She knew them all. Good men, intelligent men – but family men. Every one of them had come west at her instigation, leaving the semi-security of the crowded East in the hope of making a fortune on the plains of the Kansas range country. At her suggestion, every one of the men had sunk his savings into the town and Freddie had no wish to see them fail.

However, not one face showed a rat-like eagerness to desert a possibly sinking ship. Their town had been born – hatched might be a better word, for all hoped it would prove to be a golden egg – now all wanted to see it succeed, to grow, give them a living and become their permanent home.

"I think we're being unduly pessimistic, gentlemen," Freddie went on. "They do say that one swallow doesn't make a summer."

"Maybe not, Miss Freddie," Birnbaum replied. "But that one trail drive might make Brownton."

"Possibly," Freddie agreed. "I've something to tell you in the strictest confidence. It must not go beyond these walls. The railroad plan to run a branch line up into Montana Territory, and Philip Chaseman, he's head of construction, will build it from here or Brownton, whichever town seems most likely to succeed. I don't need to point out that the town which gets the spur line will most certainly survive and grow."

"Then we have to get the trail drive trade," Coutland stated firmly.

"How?" asked Dongelon.

"We might try sending riders out to scout for trail herds and give the news about our town," Freddie suggested. "And there's another point. The railroad don't want to run their spur line from a wild, wide-open town."

"We'll need a constable, or a marshal," Sherill said.

Any defeatist thoughts the others might have held departed as the town council settled down to discuss ways and means of gathering the trail drive trade and handling their town once customers began to flow in. After half an hour Freddie brought the meeting to a close.

"So it stands this way, gentlemen," she said. "We will have the decision from Chaseman in four weeks. I propose that we hang on until then and put our plans for steering trail drives and other trade to town into operation. All in favor?"

A chorus of "ayes" showed that the council stood unanimously behind their lady mayor. Rising from her chair, Freddie crossed the room and opened its door. A pretty little blonde girl stood before the door, bending at an angle which would have placed her eye, or ear, to the keyhole.

"I was only tying me shoelace, Miss Freddie," she gurgled, straightening up and meeting her employer's smiling eyes.

"I'm sure you were, Babsy. Tell one of the girls to bring a tray of drinks up here, then come to my bedroom and help me change."

Turning, Freddie entered the dining room and passed through it to her bedroom. After delivering her boss's orders to the bar, Babsy Smith followed Freddie and found her assistance in the capacity of maid was not required.

Mistress and maid were alike in one thing: their accents were British, not American. There any similarity ended. Freddie spoke with a cultured, upper-class accent and Babsy's voice proclaimed the fact that she had been born well within the sound of Bow Bells.

Freddie stripped off the formal black dress which went with her official position as mayor. Under it she wore a daringly brief set of black lace underwear that did nothing to hide the magnificent body under it. She stood five foot seven, with black hair that was shorter than the current fashion and an almost faultlessly beautiful face. Her breasts rose in two gorgeous globes over a slender waist that needed no corset and which rose to rounded hips and shapely legs encased in black silk stockings, the black of her suspender straps making slashes down the white flesh of her thighs. All in all Miss Freddie Woods, lady mayor of Mulrooney, was a tolerable fine piece of woman-flesh.

Opening her clothes closet, Freddie took out a skin-tight green dress which most certainly would not have done for the council's meeting – although the male members might not have objected to her wearing it. She donned the dress, it left her shoulders and arms bare and was cut low over the bosom, while a slit from floor to thigh allowed her legs to show in a pleasing and attractive manner.

Babsy looked like the kind of maid one saw in a French farce. Her blonde hair was taken up in a curly pile on top of her head and she had a pretty, mischievous and happy face with wide blue eyes that looked in a kind of open innocence at the world. Stripping off her formal – although she managed to make it look informal – maid's dress revealed that Babsy wore cheaper, but just as brief, black underwear as her mistress.

"Cor, Miss Freddie," Babsy said, throwing a glance at herself in the full-length closet mirror. "I wouldn't half like to go down the Old Kent Road in this."

"You'd be arrested before you took two steps," Freddie replied and smoothed down her frock. "I'm not exactly dressed for a hunt ball, am I?"

"You wouldn't half set the local gentry going if you showed up like it, though. Not that you didn't always, my la - Miss Freddie."

Even after eighteen months Babsy occasionally almost slipped into the old manner of addressing her mistress. Freddie threw a warning glance at her companion, although she acknowledged that she was as much to blame as Babsy with her mention of hunt balls. While the Right Honorable Lady Winifred Amelia Besgrave-Woodstole attended hunt balls, Miss Freddie Woods did not.

"How'd it go, Miss Freddie?" Babsy asked.

"I thought you heard."

"Not all of it. I was only listening to see how long you'd be. What got them all so hot under the collar?"

"The first trail drive has reached Brownton."

"Coo-er!" Babsy gasped, her wide eyes staring at her mistress. "That's bad for us, isn't it?"

"It's not good, that's for sure. If we get the trade, we get the spur line for the railroad from here. If not—"

Freddie allowed her words to trail away although she never hesitated to take Babsy into her confidence. While the little blonde could, and sometimes did, act in a feather-headed fashion, she never discussed Freddie's affairs. Babsy knew more about her mistress than any other living person. Back in England Babsy had held the minor and unimportant position of between-stairs maid, about the lowest of the low in British domestic hierarchy. Freddie picked the girl for her quick wits, courage and cheery disposition, when setting out to see some of the world. Since then she had never regretted the choice and doubted if any other of her family's retainers could have made the transition from "tweeny" to lady's maid and companion with such ease and competence. Since Freddie became a saloonkeeper, the little blonde added to her duties by proving able to get up on a stage and sing and dance in a manner much appreciated by the saloon's audiences.

"Ready?" Freddie asked on completing her clothing change.

"Yes'm."

"Let's go and see how trade is then."

"I just did," Babsy answered, her voice losing some of its merriment. "It's not good."

While walking down the stairs, Freddie looked around the large barroom of her place. One thing which caught the eye was the complete absence of male help in the room. While Freddie hired swampers, old cowhands retired from riding the range, the men rarely appeared during the hours when the saloon was open to the public. For the rest, the games of chance were run by girls Freddie had trained.

Friendly smiles and nods greeted Freddie as she crossed the room, for she was more than a boss to her girls. She acted as banker, counsellor, mother-confessor and adviser on affairs of the heart. Only once had she acted in another manner. Big Sarah, the red-haired head barmaid – Freddie's name for her female bartenders – arrived shortly after the saloon opened and stated firmly she did not intend to take orders from a fancy-talking, sissy, dude Limey. Freddie let the matter ride until after the few customers left that night, then she invited Sarah to repeat the remarks. The resulting fight lasted for half an hour, although for the last five minutes Freddie had it all her own way. Strangely, Sarah respected Freddie after the licking she took and became one of the lady saloonkeeper's stoutest supporters. The fight served two purposes: it brought Freddie a reliable boss bartender who really knew her stuff; it also warned off the other girls and none challenged Freddie's right to give them orders after seeing what happened to Big Sarah.

There was only one customer in the big saloon. The saloon drew dribbles of trade from passing trains, railroad construction workers and chance drifters. On that day only one paying guest used the room. Somehow the emptiness of the room appeared to make him look larger than life. Not that he was a small man. In fact, Freddie was willing to admit she had never seen a finer physical specimen than her solitary customer.

He would stand at least six foot three, Freddie decided as she compared him with the waitress who cleared meal things from his table and ogled him with frank admiration. On sitting down, the customer had hung his expensive white Stetson hat, its low crown and wide brim fixed Texas-style, on the back of his chair. His golden blond hair was wavy and looked newly trimmed. Studying the man's face, Freddie decided it was the most handsome she had ever seen, intelligent, strong-willed and virile as a Grecian god of old. His shoulders had a great spread to them, but he tapered down to a slim waist and long, powerful legs. In dress he spelled tophand Texas cowboy, but also something of a dandy. Freddie could tell silk when she saw it, and she saw it in the blond's tight-rolled green bandana which trailed long ends over his costly, made-to-measure tan colored shirt. All of his clothing looked expensive and he would have to buy it tailored to his giant's frame to obtain so perfect a fit, for no store would carry his sizes as a stock item. The boots and gunbelt bore the look of having been made by a master-craftsman, yet were strictly functional. While the 1860 Army Colts in the belt's contoured fast-draw holsters had ivory butts and the Best Citizens' Finish of deep blue, Freddie gained the impression that they were not worn to impress people or merely to look good.

"Adonis with the build of a Hercules," Freddie remarked, leaning on the bar and studying the big blond man.

"Huh?" grunted Big Sarah, who lacked a classical education.

"Who is he?" Freddie asked, realizing that she must have spoken her thought aloud, and turning to her head barmaid.

On the face of it, the question did not make much sense, Freddie decided. Her barmaid was unlikely to know that blond man. But Sarah did know him and her face showed some surprise that a gal as smart and knowing as her well-respected boss should profess ignorance of *that* handsome blond giant's identity.

"He ain't that Adonis feller, Miss Freddie," Sarah answered. "That there's Mark Counter. I remember him from the days when he worked as first deputy to Cap'n Dusty Fog up at Quiet Town."*

* Told in *Quiet Town* by J. T. Edson.

CHAPTER TWO

A Chance for Mulrooney

Freddie had heard both names. One could not spend time in the range country without hearing about Dusty Fog and Mark Counter. What she recalled having heard of them in connection with the Texas cattle business caused Freddie to study the blond giant with fresh interest.

Although he was the son of one of the Texas Big Bend's richest ranchers, and wealthy in his own right due to an eccentric maiden aunt leaving him all her considerable fortune in her will, Mark rode as an ordinary hand for Ole Devil Hardin's O.D. Connected ranch. Maybe not as an ordinary hand exactly, he was a member of the elite of that tough and handy crew, the floating outfit, and counted second to Dusty Fog in the ranch's hierarchy. If anything Mark could claim to be a slightly better cowhand than Dusty Fog. His strength was a legend and had built up a reputation of being a rangeland Hercules.

This then was the man who sat at a table in the Fair Lady Saloon. He might offer an answer to all Freddie's prayers concerning the development and improvement of the town.

Just as she turned from the bar, Freddie saw her place had drawn in more customers. Five in all; but they were not the sort of trade Freddie cared to attract even with the prevailing slackness of business.

They came through the batwing doors, pushing, jostling each other and generally indulging in horse-play as if they had been celebrating somewhere. If they had, it was on their own liquor for Freddie's place alone had been opened that morning. Wherever they bought it, all five appeared to be carrying a skinful of liquor and that did not make Freddie any happier to see them.

Behind the bar, Big Sarah threw a glance at the bung-starter and made sure she could get to it and the Navy Colt which lay in a box beneath the bar. Then she looked across at Mark Counter, his presence making her feel uneasy in the face of the new development. Mark was a cowhand, a good one; the five new arrivals followed the trade of buffalo hunter, although far from being in the class of Buffalo Bill Cody, Frank Mayer or other top names in their profession. Cowhands and buffalo hunters were like oil and water – flames and gun powder might be a more apt description – they just did not mix.

For a moment the five men stood just inside the door and studied the room. They all touched the six foot mark, but were lean and gaunt. Long, shaggy hair trailed from under cheap woolsey hats and none of the five appeared to have washed or shaved in a week or more. Their buckskin shirts carried so much dirt and dried buffalo blood that they might have been smelled across the width of the room, while their U.S. Cavalry pants were so encrusted with general muck that the original blue color no longer showed. Each man wore Pawnee moccasins dirty and stinking enough to turn even an Osage Indian's stomach over in disgust. Each man wore a gunbelt with a revolver at one side and a sheathed knife at the other.

"Yeeah!" yelled the man in the lead of the group, clearly their boss and in command of the revels. "Just looky in here, boys. And you all saying we ought to go to try what Brownton had to offer. Why here's a whole saloon-full of gals all eager and a-pinning for us to happy 'em up.''

"Let's grab off a gal each a-piece, Sam," answered the red-haired man at the speaker's right side. "I'll take me that black ha—"

Leaping forward with surprising speed and agility, Stokey wrapped his arms around Freddie. The stench of whisky – and not very good whisky at that – combined with the general body odor of the man almost made Freddie retch and prevented her from taking the appropriate action in her defense. All she could manage to do was twist her head away as Stokey lowered his whiskery face towards her.

"Let's have a kiss, gal," Stokey whooped. "Then we'll get us—"

Which was as far as he got without interruption. Even before Big Sarah could catch up her bung-starter and come over the counter to help Freddie, Babsy went to her mistress's aid. Ducking under Red's grabbing hands, Babsy darted forward and landed a kick across Stokey's left shin. He let out a howl like a knife-stuck fattening pig and released his hold on Freddie. Shoving the man back a pace, Freddie whipped around her right hand to drive the fist against his jaw and stagger him back a few steps. In this Stokey might have counted himself fortunate on two scores. While holding Freddie, he had swung around so his back was to the bar and went closer to it as she hit him. However, Freddie could not land her punch with full power under such cramped conditions, which was his first lucky break. Second piece of luck being that he did not go back far enough for Sarah to reach him with her bung-starter. If either condition had been more favorable to Freddie, Stokey would have wound up on the floor and wondering how so many flashing stars happened to be around his head in plain daylight.

Putting a hand to his jaw, for the blow had landed with sufficient force to hurt, Stokey let out a snarl of rage.

"You—!" he began.

"Don't say it, you drunken lout!" Freddie hissed, the cold fury glowing in her eyes. "If you can't behave in here, get out!"

Mark Counter had been studying the situation ever since it began, reaching the conclusion that he could not sit back and watch ladies—and that black-haired beauty was a real lady or he had never seen one—mishandled by a bunch of half-drunk, stinking Yankee skin-hunters.

"Like the lady said," Mark drawled, walking forward. "The door's there and the air outside's free."

For a man of some considerable experience in such matters Mark appeared to be making a bad error in his tactics. When he halted Mark stood in the center of a half-circle of buffalo hunters and it rapidly became a full circle around him.

A grin creased Stokey's face as he studied Mark and prepared to give the signal for his bunch to jump the dude-dressed Texan and hand him his needings. It would be amusing, and give the appetite a whetting for later pleasure, to work that nosey jasper over and mark him up good. Then the girls would know what kind of out-and-out, hair-on-the-chest he-men were in the saloon.

The only trouble being that Mark did not wait to be jumped on, worked over and marked up; and he had a right good and convincing argument for anybody who tried to do it.

Just as Stokey opened his mouth to give the orders, Mark moved. Suddenly shooting out his hands, Mark clamped hold of the front of Stokey's shirt and lifted the man clear from the ground. Nothing Mark could have done would have more shocked the five men than did his display of strength. It shook a man to see a feller he aimed to attack calmly lay hold of a fullgrown buffalo-hunter and heft him into the air with no more trouble or sweat than a nurse showed in lifting a baby. With Stokey held kicking and amazed in the air, Mark proceeded to deal with the other members of the buffalo-hunting quintet.

Even as the other four men started to move forward, Mark swung Stokey around in a full circle. Using the still amazed Stokey's body as a club, Mark swept three of the remaining four men from their feet, sending them sprawling as the flying body hit them. The fourth man, Scar it was, either had more agility, or less rot-gut whisky in his belly, than his friends. Whatever the reason, he made a fast leap to the rear and avoided Stokey's swinging body. Once his friend passed, Scar leapt forward to the attack once more, meaning to take Mark from the rear.

Having made his circle with Stokey for a club, Mark kindly released the man, although without placing him on the floor first. Mark had heard of the law of gravity and figured it worked equally well for buffalo hunters as it did for everything else, so Stokey would come to earth some place. Luckily for him, Stokey landed on his feet; then his luck gave out. Although on his feet, Stokey had no control of himself and teetered into the bar not a yard from where Big Sarah stood and that was tempting providence too far. Like the rest of the girls, Sarah had been staring in open-eyed amazement at Mark's display of strength, but her instincts reacted almost without command from her brain. Out came the bung-starter and whistled around to descend with a wooden "clunk!" on the top of Stokey's head. Sarah tended to be something of an expert in the skilled application of a bung-starter to a human head, knowing how to apply just enough force to render the victim helpless without cracking the skull in doing it. A glassy expression came to Stokey's face and his body crumpled forward to the saw-dust covered floor.

"Behind you," Freddie screamed as Scar sprang forward.

Having released Stokey, Mark swung around to meet the menace from the rear. Even while turning, his right shoulder bunched and propelled a hard fist forward. Too late Scar saw his danger. He tried to stop his forward movement, go back, duck or do something to avoid being hit. All to no avail he tried. Mark's hard right fist caught Scar's jaw and propelled the man backwards and over the top of a table.

Although she gave the warning, Freddie stood, like the rest of her girls, held motionless in wonder at the blond giant's display of strength. Not one of the girls gave a thought to helping Mark attend to the other three buffalo hunters.

Both the remaining men, Whiskers and Slushy to their friends, had made their feet and were attacking. A hand caught Mark's shoulder and swung him around. Whiskers' other hand crashed against Mark's jaw and staggered the blond giant into a brutal blow in the back delivered by Slushy. Grunting with pain, Mark arched his back and Whiskers, showing good teamwork with Slushy, landed a punch into Mark's stomach then whipped up a backhand drive to the Texan's face. In the same move, Slushy smashed both his hands on to the back of Mark's neck. Dazed by the blows, Mark stumbled forward and Whiskers hit him again. Mark reeled a couple of paces, caught his balance and threw a right which ripped into Whiskers' ribs and flung the surprised man sideways. That was when Whiskers' luck ran out. He landed on his knees before one of Freddie's waitresses and the girl held a stoutly made tray which she applied ringingly to the top of his head. One blow did not quite do the trick of rendering Whiskers *hors de combat*, so the girl measured him up and handed him a second blow which served its purpose.

Two hands clamped around Mark from the rear as he

dealt with Whiskers, pinning his own arms to his side. Slushy had made the move, intending to hold the big Texan helpless and allow one of his friends the opportunity of settling Mark's hash once and for all. Only Slushy struck a slight snag, one which might have filled him with a sense of frustration and panic had he been given time to think about it. His hands would barely meet around the great spread of the Texan's shoulders and arms. Before Slushy could debate the point, Mark took its solution from the other man's hands – although probably not to Slushy's satisfaction. With a sudden surge of his enormous biceps, Mark spread open Slushy's arms. Then Mark drove back his right arm, crashing its elbow with battering-ram power into Slushy's ribs. Feeling as if the entire front of his ribcage had caved in, Slushy reeled away holding his chest and twisting his face in a look of agony.

Scar, the one who had avoided being felled by Stokey's flying body in the earlier stages of the fight, made his feet just as Slushy grabbed Mark and saw a heaven-sent chance presented to him. Gripping a chair by its back, he forced himself to his feet and attacked. He swung the chair into the air, meaning to use it as a club and fell the big Texan.

Seeing Mark temporarily indisposed, Freddie took a hand at that point. She thrust Babsy gently aside and flung herself forward. As a child in England, Freddie had seen the type of football made popular at Rugby School and, being something of a tomboy, learned various moves of the game; as she proceeded to demonstrate. Her flying body crashed against Scar, arms locking around his legs in as near a perfect rugby tackle as she could manage. Some experts might have found faults with minor details of her tackle, but neither Freddie nor Scar had cause to complain at it. To the accompaniment of a ripping sound, Freddie brought Scar crashing to the floor. However, not having been designed for wear while playing rugby, her dress split from thigh to armpit along the seam. She and Scar rolled over on the floor and Babsy flung herself on to the man, followed by two more of the girls. All in all, and had he been given the choice, Scar would rather have been worked over by Mark Counter than take the hair-yanking, scratching, punching, kicking and biting mauling served out by the enraged girls.

Mark had no time to admire the view Freddie presented as she rolled free of the mound of struggling girls and their victim. Already Red was back on his feet and coming in to the attack. Still doubled over in agony, Slushy saw his chance and took it. His foot shot out, catching Mark behind the left knee. Taken by surprise, Mark felt his left leg double under him and went to his knees. He lowered his head and dived forward, ramming into Red's body and sending the man staggering back into the bar. Eager to do her part, Big Sarah moved along the bar, her trusty bung-starter gripped ready for use. However Red did not wait for her, but thrust himself forward at Mark. He walked into a punch which landed in the center of his face and flattened out his nose.

There are few things in the world as painful as a fist-broken nose. Screeching with pain, Red staggered back a couple of paces. His hand dropped and brought the revolver from its holster on his right thigh. Flame tore from the gun's barrel and the crack of a shot rang out. Mark felt as if a red-hot iron bored through the flesh of his shoulder. Shock waves sent him staggering back and he was helpless to do anything to defend himself as Red cocked the gun ready to shoot again.

Still on her knees and trying to hold her dress together around her, Freddie saw the shooting and knew Mark did not have a chance. Yet she could do nothing to help him for she did not have a gun and Big Sarah stood some distance from the Navy Colt under the bar. Long before Freddie could reach Red, it would be too late to stop him shooting.

The main doors of the saloon burst open and a tall blond-haired young Texas cowhand burst in. From her position, Freddie saw the savage look on his face as his right hand dropped to draw the Army Colt from its holster on his off thigh. Freddie had never seen a real fast gun-fighting man in action until that day and always believed that stories of their speed were exaggerated. Now she learned different. In a flickering blur of movement so fast the eye could barely follow it, the newcomer drew his right side Colt and fired. His lead ripped into Red's head, shattering it like a rotten pumpkin. Cocking his gun on the recoil, the youngster swung towards Slushy. To her horror, Freddie realized that the blond boy aimed to kill the man.

"Waco!" Mark roared.

For a few seconds the youngster stood immobile, his Colt lined on Slushy with its trigger depressed by his forefinger and the hammer drawn fully back by his thumb. One slight movement of that thumb would allow the hammer to fall, strike and explode a percussion cap, sending fire leaping into the powder of the chamber and igniting it to propel the bullet into human flesh.

It was the longest few seconds Slushy could ever remember and he doubted if he would live through them. Then the blonde boy relaxed slightly, although the gun did not swing from line.

"You all right, Mark?" he asked.

"I'll do now."

The shots had broken up the struggling pile of girls on the floor; for which Scar might have felt relieved. He looked like he had tangled with a couple of bobcats, while being hauled backwards through a clump of sharp-thorned cactus plants and after having been partly scalped by a Comanche with a blunt knife.

Gasping for breath, Babsy sat up alongside the battered buffalo hunter, let a handful of his hair fall from her fingers and looked at the man who shot Red. He was a tall, handsome youngster, although his face had a watchful, mean look. There was a good width to his shoulders and his frame looked hard and fit. From his Texas-style black Stetson to the Kelly spurs on his Justin boots, he spelled cowhand from the Lone Star State. While still in his teens, the gunbelt looked like neither an affection or a decoration and he had just proved his skill with one of his brace of Army Colts.

Having heard the shots, the town councillors came into view on the stairs and looked down at their first view of a western corpse-and-cartridge affair. Slowly the men came down the stairs, staring around the room.

"What happened, Miss Freddie?" Coutland asked.

"I'll tell you later," she replied. "Go fetch the doctor, please, Shad."

A cold, sick and empty feeling crept over Freddie as she looked at Mark Counter. One thing she felt sure about; the blond giant would be unlikely to recommend to his friends a town where he had to fight odds of five to one and wound up by being shot.

Maybe Mark Counter's presence in town had been a chance for Mulrooney to survive and attract the Texas trail drive trade – but those five drunken buffalo hunters had ruined that same chance for Freddie's town.

CHAPTER THREE

Brownton's Chance

"Be it known that all persons who served the Confederate States during the late War of Secession are required and ruled by Brownton City Civic Ordinance No. 28 to surrender their firearms to the office of Town Marshal Banks Fagan on arrival in the city limits and not to wear or carry any firearms during their stay in the said city limits.

Signed,
B. A. Grief, *Mayor.*"

Although the sign hung prominently on the wall of Kate Gilgore's Buffalo Saloon, neither of the two young men who entered showed any interest in it beyond a first casual glance. Yet both could read, one of them slowly and as long as there were not too many long words and the other very well – and both had weapons on their persons.

One of the pair might be termed extra well armed, especially in view of his apparent youth, for, in addition to the walnut handled old Dragoon Colt hanging butt forward at his right side, he had a bowie knife sheathed at the left and a Winchester Model of 1866 rifle in his left hand.

While he appeared to be around sixteen years old, it must be admitted that in the Ysabel Kid's case the looks were deceptive. He was older than sixteen and had packed a world of practical savvy into every year of his life. It was his face that gave the impression of youth, being innocent-looking and almost babyishly handsome – unless one looked at his cold, wolf-savage red-hazel eyes. They were not the eyes of a sixteen-year-old boy. All his clothing from hat, through bandana, shirt and levis down to his boots, was black; only the brown walnut grips of the old Second Model Dragoon Colt and the ivory grips of the James Black bowie knife relieved the blackness.

There was something wild, alien, almost Indian about the Ysabel Kid. One way of accounting for this stemmed from his mother being a French Creole-Comanche girl with direct bloodline to Chief Long Walker of the dreaded Dog Soldier Lodge, while his father had been a wild Irish Kentuckian who loved to fight and had sand to burn. The Kid came from fighting stock on both sides. He handled a rifle like a backwoodsman of old, used his knife with the flair of both French Creole and Comanche – knife fighters from way back, could use his Dragoon with some skill although not well enough to be termed a gun-fighter. Mostly the Kid handled scouting work for the O.D. Connected spread; and in addition to being able to move in silence over sun-dried sticks or capable of following tracks where a buck Apache would give up, he spoke several Indian dialects well and fluent Spanish. Not a bad record for a man who lacked formal education. All in all the Ysabel Kid made a good friend, but a bad, mean enemy.

That then was the Ysabel Kid; his companion being none other than the Rio Hondo gun wizard Dusty Fog. How would one expect such a man as Dusty Fog to look?

He had been a Confederate Army captain at seventeen and his name ranked with John Singleton Mosby or Turner Ashby as a *fighting* Calvalry commander. The union Army respected him as a shrewd and gallant enemy; and the man who rode behind their lines to give evidence at a court martial, clearing a Yankee lieutenant wrongly accused of cowardice.* After the war, Dusty's name rose high as a cowhand, the segundo of the great O.D. Connected ranch and a master trail driver. He was also the man who tamed and brought law to Quiet Town when that Montana city rolled high, wild and woolly. Men told much of his skill in a bare-handed fight; but mostly they spoke of his chain-lightning draw and deadly accuracy, claiming him to be the fastest of that magic-handed group produced by conditions in Texas after the war.

Such a man ought to be a veritable handsome giant amongst men.

Dusty Fog stood five foot six in his high-heeled, expensive cowhand boots. While his clothing cost as much as Mark Counter's, Dusty did not have the flair to show it off to its best advantage. At first glance Dusty might have been passed over as a small, insignificant Texas cowhand; good looking and with dusty blond hair, but not noticeable enough to rate a closer study. Happen one did look closer, there was a strength and intelligence in Dusty's face, his grey eyes met a scrutiny without any flinching. His muscular development would have equalled Mark Counter's had they both been the same height; but few folks noticed that any more than they noticed the matched brace of Army Colts in the contoured holsters of a real well-made gunbelt – until either the strength or use of his guns became necessary. Once a person saw Dusty in action, he or she never again thought of the Rio Hondo gun wizard as being small.

After glancing around the room, Dusty turned to the bartender. "Take two beers," he ordered, "and have something youself."

Buffalo Kate Gilgore's employees had none of the usual Kansas trail end town antipathy towards the

---

* Told in *The Fastest Gun in Texas* by J. T. Edson.

Texans who supplied the butter to put on their bread, so the bartender decided to hand out a warning before it became too late.

"Sign there means what it says, friend," he remarked, nodding to the wall.

Resting his "yellow boy" rifle – so named because of its brass frame – on the bar top, the Kid gave a grin. "Saw me a whole slew of fellers wearing guns as we rode in."

"Yeah? Well they live here."

"And that gives them, and not us, the right to benefit by the Second Amendment?" asked Dusty.

"Huh?" grunted the bartender.

"The Second Amendment of the United States Constitution, friend," Dusty explained. "It goes something like 'A well regulated militia being necessary to the security of a free state, the right of the people to keep and bear arms shall not be infringed.' "

"Which same, comes last herd count, me'n' Dusty was marked down as being people," the Kid went on. "So we come under the Second Amendment."

"But the—"

"Pour out the beers, friend," Dusty interrupted. "Say, whose turn is it to pay, Lon?"

"Danged if I don't have to go out back," the Kid replied and took up his rifle, heading for the door at the rear of the room.

"Never once knowed it to fail," Dusty grinned, watching his *amigo* walk away. "Mention paying and he takes off like a wolf-chased pronghorn antelope."

Throwing a worried look around the saloon, the bartender poured out three drinks. He had given out a serious warning and hoped the small Texan might take it. There were only a few railroad workers, awaiting a train to the construction camps, present. The bartender could better have understood Dusty's attitude had he recognized the small Texan, or had there been a large bunch of Texans in town to back up his play should a showdown come. One small, insignificant young feller and bald-faced boy would not have much chance against Fagan and his three deputies.

Thinking of the devil may not produce him; but it is a fact that as the bartender gave thought of Fagan's deputies, one of them walked by the window of the saloon, glancing in. For a moment the bartender thought, hoped even, that big Vince Crocker had missed noticing the small Texan. However, on reaching the doors, the deputy thrust them open and entered. For a moment he stood looking around him and then walked forward across the room to halt behind Dusty. There was quite a contrast between the two men for Crocker stood six foot two and had a decent, though not exceptional, build that towered over Dusty.

"The guns, cow-nurse," Crocker growled.

Slowly Dusty turned and looked the man over. "I'm just passing through, don't aim to stop on."

A sly grin came to Crocker's face. A jerk of his head sent the bartender out of ear-shot. While having nothing against the small Texan, the bartender had to go on living in Brownton; a thing which would not be easy or pleasant to do with Fagan's deputies regarding him as being uncooperative.

"Finish your drink then, feller," Crocker told Dusty in a low voice; but as Dusty turned back to do so the deputy yelled, "Don't try it!"

Out lashed Crocker's fist in a blow at Dusty's head; a blow powered to hurt the small Texan, make him angry enough to grab for his gun but dazed enough to be easy meat for Crocker's Colt. The trouble was that the blow failed to connect. Dusty completed his turn, dropping forward on to his hands upon the floor. Coiling up his legs under him, Dusty kicked back with them, driving his boots into Crocker's stomach. The big deputy yelped in pain and reeled back a few steps, holding his middle.

After delivering the unexpected kick, Dusty bounded to his feet and turned to face Crocker, waiting to see what the deputy aimed to try next.

After rubbing his stomach, Crocker lunged forward once more. He decided against shooting down the small Texan – at least, not until he had worked the short runt over. Again Crocker's fist lashed out and once more it failed to connect.

Dusty turned his back on the man, hunching his shoulders and head forward as if trying to avoid the blow. The very attitude threw Crocker off guard and set him up for what came next. Suddenly Dusty fell forward, landing on his stomach, so that Crocker's advancing left foot descended between his open legs. Rolling on to his back, Dusty pressed forward with his left leg and forced against Crocker's trapped limb with his right shin. For a moment Crocker tried to keep his balance, then went down, landing on his belly with a gratifying – to Dusty's ears – thud. Immediately the deputy landed, Dusty sat up and caught the toe of Crocker's left boot in his left hand. Then Dusty bent Crocker's trapped limb over his right leg, forcing down on the gripped toe as if trying to press it on to the deputy's backbone.

Pain knifed through Crocker's trapped leg, causing him to yell and struggle in an attempt to free himself. The contortions of the big deputy's body allowed his handcuffs to slip from his pocket. Bending forward, Dusty released the trapped leg with one hand and gathered up the handcuffs. After opening them, without losing his hold on Crocker, Dusty put them down close to hand. As Crocker tried to grab Dusty, the small Texan caught his wrist. Holding the deputy with his legs, Dusty snapped one link of the handcuffs on to the captured wrist and secured the other to the bar's brass foot-rail. Then he released Crocker and came to his feet.

At that moment Fagan's other two deputies entered the saloon. They had been making their rounds and stepped in as a matter of routine. Coming to a halt as if they had struck an invisible wall, the two men stared at the scene before them. A low curse left Stock's lips and his hand started to move towards the ivory butted Colt at his right side. At the bar Dusty's hands crossed in a flickering blur of movement, bringing his matched guns out, their hammers clicking back under his thumbs as they left leather. Knowing something of Fagan and his deputies' way of upholding the law, Dusty did not wait to discover their full intentions. Way he saw it, the discovery could best be made *after* his long barrelled Army Colts covered the two men.

"That was what I call *real* fast," Kady Jones said calmly.

"Just stand good and still," Dusty replied.

Having been a professional gunfighter before taking on the post of deputy to Fagan, Kady Jones had no intention of doing other than standing still. He knew such smoothly efficient speed only rarely failed to be accompanied by an equal accuracy of placing home bullets where they would do most good. Being younger, and full of the feeling of importance and power association with Banks Fagan gave him, Stock failed to show such good sense or as clear a grasp of the true merits of the situation. So he made a suggestion which sent a cold finger running down Jones' spine.

"He can't get both of us, Kady. Let's take him."

"You get him to promise he'll handle you first, and I'm game to try," the gaunt gunfighter replied. "Otherwise I'm fixing in to do just what this gent wants me to do."

For all his cynical comment Jones knew the suggestion had some, though not much merit. Given but one slight hint of inattention on the Texan's part, even one of only a split-second, and Jones would take his chances on his lightning fast draw.

Then, even as Jones thought things over, the matter was taken clean out of his hands. It went to the ac-

companiment of a double clicking sound unique to a
Winchester rifle as its cocking lever fed a round into the
chamber. The sound drew both deputies' eyes to where
the Ysabel Kid lounged at the saloon's door, his old
"yellow boy" held in what soldiers called the "high
port" position enabling a skilled user to bring his rifle
into action fast; nothing in the Kid's attitude and appearance hinted that he might not be a skilled user of a
rifle. Having arrived unnoticed at about the same time
as the two deputies, and read the facts of the scene with
commendable speed, the Kid took a hand.

The fact that Dust Fog had thrown down on and
covered a brace of prime town law badges meant
nothing to the Kid. Way he looked at it, Dusty had a
right good reason for such an action. Even if Dusty did
not have a good reason for showing such disrespect for
the law, the Kid would still have backed him as became
a good, true and loyal friend.

"Good question now'd be what started this," Jones
remarked.

Suddenly Crocker lunged forward, his free arm
shooting out in an attempt to catch Dusty's ankle.
However before he could reach the small Texan, the
handcuff brought him to a jarring halt, instead of
sliding along the rail.

"You never was better'n half-smart, Vince," Jones
said calmly. "That feller made sure you couldn't get
close to him. Just lie still a whiles and let us talk things
out." He looked at Dusty. "Like to tell me your side,
mister?"

"Sure," Dusty replied. "Do we call it a truce?"

"A truce she is."

On receiving Jones' agreement, Dusty holstered his
Colts and the Kid lowered his rifle although he kept
three fingers through the cocking lever, forefinger on
the trigger and thumb coiled around the small of the
butt.

Jones relaxed; but Stock grabbed at his gun's butt.

While the young deputy reckoned to be fast – and expected Jones to back his play – he had tangled in the wrong company. Like the flickering strike of an enraged rattlesnake, Dusty's left hand stabbed out, crossing his body and fetching the right side Colt from leather. Even as Stock's Colt cleared leather, Dusty fired. The young deputy gave a scream as a bullet drove into his knee-cap. His leg caved under him and he went to the ground, half-fainting in the agony and, fortunately for him, letting the gun fall from his hand.

Strange as it may seem, the Ysabel Kid – that wolf-cautious and suspicious-natured young man – made no attempt to lift his rifle and cover Jones.

"Is that how your friends keep their truces?" Dusty asked.

"Fool kid," Jones answered, seeing Dusty exonerated him of all blame. "He made the move, not me."

The door of a side room flew open and a man burst out, hand reaching for a gun. He was a big, burly man wearing range clothes and sporting the badge of town marshal on his vest. Sliding to a halt, he stopped his hand falling for he looked into the muzzle of Dusty's Colt.

"Take him, Jones," the man ordered.

"You can't see the other one, Banks," Jones replied.

Banks Fagan scowled. Like any proficient fighting man, he knew when to sing low and yell "calf rope". A low curse left his lips as he took in the situation, realizing two of his men were out of action and his best gun had been taken out of the jackpot.

"You'll not get away with this," Fagan warned.

"Which same your two deputies tried real hard to prove," Dusty replied. "If I put up my gun, do I get to talk this time?"

Two more shapes appeared at the door of the room. One of them was a tall, portly, sly-looking man wearing costly town clothes that looked a mite too good for him. The other, a woman, attracted only a brief glance from

Dusty. She stood maybe five foot seven and had a buxom, yet firm-fleshed figure. Blonde hair piled on top of her head; her face bore some make-up, though not too much. From the blue dress she wore, revealing rather than concealing her figure, Dusty figured her to be Buffalo Kate Gilgore, owner of the saloon.

"What's all this, Marshal Fagan?" boomed the big man, in a real hand-shaking politician's voice, starting to step forward.

"Just stay right where you are, mister!" Dusty snapped.

Coming to a halt, Mayor Baxter A. Grief scowled at the small Texan. After being mayor of two western towns, he possessed a fair working knowledge of such situations. Counting on the reluctance of most men to shoot down an unarmed person, Grief had planned to step between Fagan and Dusty, allowing the marshal a chance to draw and shoot. The trouble with Grief's plan being that Dusty saw through it and brought it to a halt before it could be started.

"You'll never get out of town alive," Grief warned. "Put up your gun and I'll see you get a fair trial."

Dusty saw Buffalo Kate give a warning head-shake that was certainly not directed at any of the local talent. Emotions warred on the woman's friendly, jovial and good-looking face. Clearly she wanted to lend the small Texan a helping hand, but knew what her fate would be at Fagan's hands if she did. So, beyond giving the one warning, she decided to leave matters in Dusty's capable hands.

"Sure," Dusty drawled. "We'd get a fair trial, then you'd hang us – unless we were shot trying to escape on the way to jail."

"This's Marshal Banks Fagan from Dakota!" Grief spluttered.

"Which same's more reason for not putting up the gun," Dusty answered. "I've heard about him."

From the way he spoke, Dusty had heard little good

about Marshal Banks Fagan of Dakota Territory.

Just as Fagan thought of calling on every man in the saloon to help him, deputizing them as was his right under the law, a man walked in through the batwing doors. Despite his fashionable eastern clothes, the man showed a remarkably quick grasp of the western situation before him. Coming to an abrupt halt, he took in the barroom's scene with a quick glance and kept his hands well clear of his jacket. After sweeping the room, the man's eyes came to rest on Dusty and a look of surprise came to his face.

"Cap'n Fog," he said. "What's all this?"

The way Grief's mouth dropped open at the words, it was lucky he had a neck in the way to stop it. Part of the mayor's duties in Brownton was to know important visitors and make sure their stay be as welcome and happy as possible. The newcomer rated top priority treatment, he was Waldo Burkman, head cattle-buyer for a big eastern company and a man who could bring thousands of dollars into Brownton. And he clearly recognized the small Texan – more than that, he used a name Grief had heard many times. Nor was Burkman likely to be making jokes at such a moment, pretending the small Texan was somebody he was not.

"What happened?" Fagan asked.

"Your deputy came in and pulled the old resisting arrest game on me," Dusty replied. "Grabbed me over the poster there, then told me to finish my drink. Only he spoke so low that nobody but me could hear. Then he yelled out and threw a punch at me. I figured he'd be safer down there for a spell."

Fagan knew Crocker very well and did not doubt that Dusty told the truth about the deputy's earlier actions. Yet he wondered how a small man like the Texan managed to put Crocker in such a position. The answer was simple. Down in the Rio Hondo, working as servant to Ole Devil Hardin, lived a small man who looked Chinese but boasted of coming from some place called

Nippon. From this man Dusty learned two fighting arts, ju-jitsu and karate, strange to the Western world but ideally suited to offset his lack of inches, Crocker knew none of this, nor did his boss, but the deputy could, and later did, profanely testify to its effectiveness.

"How about Bell?" Fagan asked, deciding to drop the Crocker side of the affair.

"Jones called a truce so we could talk things out. I agreed, put up my guns, and Bell tried to draw. He didn't make it."

Once again Fagan guessed that Dusty told the simple truth. Young Bell Stock had a sneaky, mean streak in him when given the right kind of backing; and he probably figured Kady Jones to be backing enough. The ruined condition of his leg showed how wrong he had been.

"Anything more, Marshal?" Dusty asked after a pause in which nobody said anything at all.

"No!" The word came out bitter as bile from Fagan's lips. He did not doubt the full story would be spread around town before nightfall.

"Let's go, Lon."

Not until he received the word from Dusty did the Kid relax. The two Texans walked acrosss the saloon and Burkman followed in their heels.

Hurrying out of the room, Grief halted on the sidewalk and watched the two Texans riding out of town. He turned to Burkman and put on an ingratiating smile.

"Did Captain Fog say when his trail drive would be arriving?"

A cold smile flickered across Burkman's face.

"Yes," he replied; "it won't be arriving at all."

"W – won't—!"

"That's what I said. Well, I'll be going. I want to draw my money from the bank and catch the afternoon train down to Mulrooney."

CHAPTER FOUR

Now Ask Me the Other Question

"I'm pleased to meet you, Captain Fog," Freddie Woods smiled, holding out her hand.

Dusty had ridden into Mulrooney after meeting Waco on the Brownton trail and hearing the youngster's account of the happenings in the Fair Lady Saloon. After a profane, but admiring description of the way Freddie and her girls helped Mark deal with the buffalo hunters, Waco went on to tell how he followed Stokey's bunch out and well clear of Mulrooney before swinging around to look for Dusty on the Brownton trail. From the way Waco spoke, he reckoned Mulrooney to be an all-right town and that Freddie was a real, for-sure lady.

For her part, Freddie had a shrewd judgment of human nature and saw beneath the small, yet powerful frame to the real big man beyond it.

"My pleasure, ma'am," Dusty answered formally, feeling the strength in the girl's hand. "How's Mark?"

"I called in Doctor Brennan to attend to his wound. Come up and see the patient for yourself."

On following Freddie upstairs to one of the first floor rooms, Dusty found Mark to be doing all right. The blond giant lay in a comfortable bed, his shoulder bandaged and his back propped up with soft pillows, while one of Freddie's best-looking girls sat at his side having brought him a tray of delicacies.

"Well?" asked Freddie when she and Dusty left the sick room.

"I'd say very well," Dusty replied with a grin. "I'll be lucky to get him back on his feet this year."

Showing Dusty into her suite of rooms, Freddie told him to make himself at home and went to order a meal. Dusty looked around the well-furnished room.

"Admiring my armory?" Freddie asked, entering the room.

"Yes, ma'am."

"What do you use?"

"A Winchester carbine. It's one of the earliest the company brought out. I was given it by their representative for helping him deliver a consignment to Juarez in Mexico."*

Freddie guessed that there was more to the story than that, but did not ask any questions. A smile came to her face as she watched Dusty lift one of the duelling swords from the case.

Taking the second sword, Freddie moved back a little and, adopting a ready position, said, "*En garde!*"

On the heels of the words, she lunged with the button-tipped sword. Much to her surprise, Dusty deflected her blade and, with a quick *riposte* drove his own sword out to hit her. Nor did luck account for the hit. Dusty had adopted a near classic on guard position and handled the sword with deft ease.

"You've used a sword before," Freddie accused.

"Back in the War I learned which end to hold and which to poke with," Dusty replied.

"We must try a few passes when I'm more suitably dressed," she told him, guessing that his knowledge went far beyond the limitations he set.

"Any time you say, ma'am," Dusty answered.

The arrival of a meal prevented further discussion, or

* Told in *The Ysabel Kid* by J. T. Edson.

arrangements for future fencing matches. After living on stew, beef and beans – the trial crews' usual food – since leaving Texas, Dusty sat down with an excellent appetite to a really well-cooked meal. Freddie hired a good cook and consequently conversation during the meal did not flourish.

"You may smoke," Freddie told Dusty over their coffee.

"Do you?" Dusty asked.

"My grandmother used to," smiled Freddie. "She let me try, but it made me sick. Waco says you've a good sized herd."

"Three thousand, four hundred and sixty head last trail count."

"That's a lot of cattle," Freddie remarked.

"Sure, but there's a market for them back East."

A sudden chilling sensation hit Freddie at Dusty's words as she realized there was not a single cattle buyer in town. She could imagine Dusty's thoughts if he should bring his herd to Mulrooney and then discover there was no way he might sell it. Of course there was a chance she might contact a buyer in – no, the citizens of Brownton would never pass on a message asking a buyer to leave their town at the request of their hated rivals down the railroad track.

"When will your herd arrive?" she asked.

"This evening, before sundown most likely."

For a moment Freddie thought of asking the banker to buy the herd and keep it until such time as a cattle buyer arrived. However she saw the futility of such a suggestion. Coutland could hardly afford to allow such a large sum of money to leave his establishment, especially as Freddie did not know how long it might be before a buyer arrived. There was only one honorable way out of the mess.

"Dusty, there isn't a cattle buyer in town."

The words came out with only a trace of Freddie's bitter disappointment showing in them. Of all the rotten luck to hit a girl, this was clearly the worst. First to meet a trail boss, make a favorable impression on him, and then have to admit he could not sell his herd in her town.

"Isn't, huh?" Dusty asked.

"No."

"That's life. How about showing me around your town?"

"Of course," Freddie agreed, being too good a hostess to deny her guest anything. "Let me change first."

On passing through the saloon, they collected Waco. One of Freddie's old swampers had visited the livery barn and the girl's dainty spot-rumped Appaloosa gelding stood saddled and waiting at the hitching rail next to the three Texans' horses. Freddie smiled as she saw that Waco rode a paint stallion which matched Dusty's in size; she guessed the youngster selected such a horse because Dusty went against the rangeland prejudice at paints for working mounts.

"Would you like to see the jail?" she asked.

"You're taking us on the grand tour," Dusty answered.

"Not me," Waco drawled; "I always reckon looking's right likely to be catching."

"You've been listening to Lon," Dusty remarked.

"Why sure. He makes right good sense – sometimes."

"Take Mark's horse to the herd then," Dusty ordered. "Come in with it."

"Yo!" the youngster said, doffed his hat to Freddie and then sent his paint loping off at a good speed, leading Mark's huge bloodbay stallion by its reins.

"He's a nice youngster," Freddie remarked. "Have you known him long?"

"Not long. We ran into some trouble down on the Indian Nations line and he helped us handle it. He's got sand to burn and there's a real good brain in his head. Good hand with cattle.''

"And with a gun.''

"That too. He was left an orphan in a Waco Indian raid, almost from birth. A settler took him in, had nine kids of his own, but made Waco feel just like one of the family. Only the boy had itching feet and took to roaming. He's a natural with a gun; most kids can shoot before they can read and write down to Texas and he had a gun almost from the time he was old enough to tote one. When I met him he was riding with Clay Allison's C.A. and neither man nor boy rides with Clay unless they can handle a gun.''

"Why did he leave Allison?'' Freddie asked.

"Clay figured Waco was getting too much like him. Figured he deserve better than being a trigger-fast-and-up-from-Texas kid, which is what he was getting to be, so asked if I'd take him along with me. I agreed.''

There was much more to the story than that. A few weeks before meeting Waco, Dusty's younger brother, working as a Texas Ranger, had been killed and the youngster looked much like Danny Fog. Only Waco had been developing into a fast-gun killer with a log-sized chip on his shoulder. Then Dusty saved Waco when the youngster's horse fell before a stampede.* Since that day, Waco had followed Dusty and given the small Texan an almost dog-like devotion. His character was already changing; refraining from shooting down more than one buffalo hunter proved that.

"Does he have another name?''

"Not that I, or he, knows of. The folks who raised him never troubled to adopt him formally. Folks began by calling him the Waco-orphaned baby and in time it became shortened to Waco. One thing I do know, one

_____

* Told in *Trigger Fast* by J. T. Edson.

name or so many it would cover a tally book's page, there's a real good man inside that boy.''

"I see," Freddie said. "Would you like to look over the jail?"

Lack of experience or not, the jail had been stoutly constructed. Its front half had been given over to three offices, one at the right for the marshal; the room at the left, Freddie explained, for a county sheriff's deputy if the sheriff got around to sending one.

Looking at the central office, Dusty was reminded of Quiet Town, or his father's jail down in the Rio Hondo country. Facing the main doors stood the usual big desk, as yet unscarred by cigarette ends or spur-decorated boot heels, its log book closed and unused. The bulletin board had a few wanted posters tacked on it, but the stove was unlit. To the right of the rear wall's door stood a safe and on the left was a rack for shoulder weapons but as yet this was empty.

"One of my swampers acts as jailer," Freddie remarked.

"Huh huh!" Dusty grunted. "How about handcuffs and leg irons?"

"In the desk cupboard."

Opening the cupboard door, Dusty lifted out the tools of restraint and examined them, nodding his approval. He put them back again and looked at Freddie.

"Well?" she asked.

"You bought good stock. It pays in the long run."

"We were wondering about rifles," the girl went on, indicating the empty rack. "I thought of buying half-a-dozen Winchesters."

"Good guns," Dusty admitted.

"The best repeating rifles ever made," Freddie said in a casual tone.

"Sure."

"All right, darn you! What's your opinion?"

"Of the Winchester, or the jail's armament?"

"The latter," Freddie answered, icily calm.

"Was I you, I'd stock up with twin barrel, ten-gauge shotguns. Get them with twenty inch barrels if you can, but not longer than twenty-four. Throw in a couple of Winchesters later when the fines start coming in."

"Shotguns?"

"Sure. They're the finest argument I know for town use. A sheriff's office works out on the range, needs guns that will carry further than a revolver, but a marshal's jurisdiction ends with the civic limits. In town the range's likely to be short and a shotgun's a mighty good convincer should one be needed."

"I see."

"Tell you though," Dusty went on. "A good buffalo gun such as Remington or Sharps put out is worth having."

"But you said—"

"Which only goes to prove that you can't trust Texans," Dusty interrupted Freddie's interruption. "Seriously though, Freddie, a buffalo gun gives the user range, power and accuracy. Was I you, I'd go for one Sharps or Remington even before you buy Winchesters."

"Why?" she asked, knowing that Dusty had considerable experience in such matters and wishing to learn all she could.

"There are times, even in town, when having a rifle that holds true at half a mile – which a Winchester won't – can save lives. Say you've got a bad *hombre* holed up someplace; a man with a long-range rifle can maybe get him where it could cost the lives of two – three good men taking him at shorter range. I know that it sounds cold-blooded—"

"But necessary," Freddie answered. "I'm afraid I'm not one of those ideologic idiots who pretend they believe that the life of some thief or killer is of more importance to the community than that of an honest law enforcement officer. Would you like to see the rear of the building?"

"Why sure," Dusty smiled and opened the rear door.

The more he saw of Miss Freddie Woods, the better he liked her; and her views on the relative importance of human life matched his own.

The rear section of the jail showed the same careful planning and attention to detail as did the front. Freddie pointed to the three cells with steel barred doors and which could be used to accommodate the usual crop of minor offenders fetched in each night. In either end of the triple cells was a smaller room with a stout wooden door that had a small barred grill in it; these would house dangerous prisoners. Beyond the cells lay the marshal and deputies' night-duty accommodation and, built into a separate segment, a couple of cells and a small room where women prisoners could be held and searched.

"And you say that nobody in town has had any experience?" Dusty asked as he and Freddie left the rear of the building.

"That's right."

"Then who designed all this?"

"I did. Is it all right?"

"Stop fishing for compliments," he told her. "This's as neat a lay-out as I've ever seen."

"I just did what I thought would be needed," Freddie replied, trying to keep the pride out of her voice. "Come on, I'll show you the stock pens."

"Why sure," Dusty agreed, wondering if the stock pens were as well-designed as the rest of the town.

"Are cowhands really as wild as one hears, Dusty?" Freddie asked as they mounted their horses before the jail.

"We like to have our fun," he answered.

"Riding and shooting?"

"In most cases about the only thing a cowhand owns is his horse and his gun. So when he plays, that's what he plays with. When he's got pay in his pocket, he acts a mite rowdy."

"Hoorawing the town, don't they call it?"

"That's one way," Dusty agreed. "One trouble is that when he sees a town he gets a mite excited, especially after a drive."

For the rest of the ride to the stock pens Dusty told Freddie of cattle trailing. He painted a graphic picture of what went into walking a herd of half-wild longhorn cattle from Texas to Kansas; explaining how the hands worked anywhere from ten to twenty-four hours a day, braved the elements, risked storm, flood, drought, Indian attack and stampede. Never had Dusty talked as he did with Freddie and at the end of the time she had gained an insight into cowhand mentality and knew why the hands behaved a mite wildly when they finally discharged their burden at the shipping pens.

More than ever before Freddie realized the enormity of the task ahead of her. While her inborn sense of justice and fair play would not allow her to discriminate against the cowhands, she wanted to make sure they kept their high spirits within reasonable bounds.

While showing Dusty the stock pens, Freddie wondered how she might establish some control over the trail crews, buffalo hunters, railroad workers and the folk who flocked in to prey on those who came to town. Then she remembered that she first must attract the cowhands to her town. Not until that happened would Freddie need to bother about keeping the peace.

For a time Dusty sat his horse and studied the stock pens in silence, letting the girl have her thoughts unbroken. In his imagination he saw how the cattle could be passed into the big pens alongside the track and out on to the waiting cars. From what Dusty could see, the operation would be smoother and easier than in any other town he had visited.

"Who designed them?" he asked.

"Mil Sanders, down to the depot," Freddie replied. "Are they all right?"

"They'll do real well. We can start shoving the herd

straight in when it arrives this evening.''

"Of co—" Freddie began, then almost groaned aloud. "But there aren't any cattle-buyers in town."

"Didn't I tell you?" asked Dusty innocently. "I saw Waldo Burkman in Brownton and arranged for him to meet me down here."

Freddie could not speak for almost a minute, but from the way her face turned red she sure wanted to. All the time she had been worrying herself into a tizzy – Freddie often wondered at the way she picked up western terms – and that white-topped *big* man from Texas knew she did not need to worry at all.

"Oooh!" she finally managed to gasp, and if she had been on the ground she would have stamped up a war-dance. "Oooh! Just you wait, Dusty Fog!"

"Did I do something wrong?" he answered mildly, and before she could tell him, went on, "I sent word down trail to warn every drive moving north about what to expect in Brownton. Your town might get some of the drives that were headed there."

"Dusty," Freddie said, her voice husky. "I – you – I don't know how to thank you."

"For what? Going to look over a town, learning that it stinks worse than a six day dead stunk-up skunk and sending a warning to other Texans. Happen you want to thank me, just run one Kansas town where a Texan doesn't get cheated blind."

"I'll try to do it," she promised.

On the way back to town Freddie turned the subject to law enforcement. Once again Dusty told her much about the work a lawman in a western town, especially such a town as Mulrooney, would find himself doing. Freddie fired question after question at Dusty and so absorbed did she become that they rode straight by the front of her place.

"Where now, Kansas City, Hays, or your home in England?" Dusty inquired as they left town.

"To my pl—Have we passed it?"

"One thing's for sure, it didn't up and walk away."

Turning their horses, they rode back into town again. Freddie sank into her thoughts, turning over and over the problem of policing Mulrooney. One thing was for sure, handling the law in her town would take a special kind of man. There were a number of professional lawmen in Kansas Territory, the Earp brothers, Wild Bill Hickok and their kind, but Freddie did not care to hire them for all were violently anti-Texan and hated cowhands – and, if rumor be true, none too honest. Freddie swore that Mulrooney would have honest law and finally handed the problem to Dusty.

"There's a good feller down in the Indian Nations, Kail Beauregard's his name. His works with Bill Tilghman and Billy'd supply references happen you needed them. Kail'd be just what you want. He knows soldiers, cowhands, buffalo hunters and western towns."

"How long would it be before he arrives?" Freddie asked.

"Four or five weeks at the earliest."

"Oh!"

Freddie's flat, one-worded reply showed the world of disappointment. Long before Kail Beauregard could arrive, her town would have a reputation for being wild, woolly and full of fleas. The railroad would not run their spurline to Montana from a lawless town.

Reaching out his hand, Dusty caught Freddie's horse by the bridle and halted it before her place. Then he grinned at her and said, "Now ask me the other question Freddie gal."

"Which other question's that?" she inquired.

"Will I run the law for you until Kail Beauregard arrives."

For a long moment Freddie did not reply. Then she shook her head and stared at Dusty with admiration in her eyes.

"Remind me never to play cards with you," she said. "I used to think I had a pretty fair poker face."

"Let's put it that I made a lucky guess," Dusty replied. "Where do we leave the horses?"

"At the livery barn. But I can't impose on your good-nature any more."

"Tell you what," grinned Dusty. "You tell Lon and the boys that I've got a good nature, and I'll run the law for you until Kail gets up here."

"Captain Fog, sir," Freddie answered, holding out her hand. "You have just made yourself a deal – if the town council agree to it."

"Reckon they will?"

"I just reckon they might," Freddie smiled. "Like you, I can be mighty persuasive when I need to be."

Freddie felt happier than she had for days as she rode into the livery barn with Dusty Fog. It seemed that her troubles were coming to an end. With Dusty handling the law, nothing serious could go wrong. At last she could settle down and run her saloon in peace.

Which might have come true if Buffalo Kate Gilgore stayed out of Mulrooney.

CHAPTER FIVE

Payoff for O.D. Connected

Word flew around Mulrooney like the wind-fanned flames of a range fire. Soon everyone in town knew a trail herd was coming and would arrive before sundown. The afternoon eastbound train brought in a number of well-dressed men who made for Coutland's bank and deposited thick wads of money as well as certified cheques for large sums; they were the cattle buyers coming to meet the herds, for word of Dusty Fog's departure from Brownton had gone the rounds and the buyers guessed what action he would take. After visiting the bank, the buyers headed for the Fair Lady Saloon where they bidded against each other for the herd and it finally went to Burkman's company at a near record price of forty-eight dollars a head.

Almost everybody in town went out to the stock pens to see the arrival of the first herd. Dusty and Burkman arrived with Freddie and most of the local dignitaries gathered around to meet the young man who was responsible for saving their town. People studied Dusty with interest and a hundred different stories of his life or capabilities made the rounds. Dusty warned the crowd to keep well back from the stock pens; especially those on foot, for a longhorn feared human beings only as long as they sat on horseback.

Time passed by and every eye watched the dot appear on the distant rim, extend into a long, winding line and take the form of the approaching herd.

Sitting her Appaloosa alongside Dusty and Burkman, Freddie watched the mile-long column of cattle with its flanking riders around it. Behind the herd came the remuda of spare horses for the trail hands and bringing up the rear rolled the men's mobile home, the chuck and bed wagons. It made a breathtaking scene, the more so when one remembered the journey the herd had made to reach Mulroony.

A tall young man raced his big claybank stallion from the front of the herd, making for Dusty's party. Under his shoved-back brown hat, a mass of curly, fiery red hair framed a freckled, pugnaciously-handsome face that looked made to hold a broad grin. He wore trail-dirty cowhand clothes and a brace of walnut handled Army Colts rode butt forward in his holsters.

"Here they are, Dusty," he whooped, sliding the horse to a halt.

"Why sure," Dusty agreed. "You made it, Cousin Red. Uncle Devil'll be real pleased when he hears."

To Freddie it seemed that the young man's chest expanded several inches at Dusty's words. Certainly Red Blaze felt considerable pride in his achievement. The trouble was that Red tended to jump into any fight he came across, helping the weaker side without finding what caused the trouble, so most folks figured him to be a mite wild and irresponsible. Dusty knew different. Give Red a job to do, or put him in a position of trust, and he became the most cool of men. The way he had handled the trail drive in Dusty's absence proved that.

"You know Waldo, I reckon, Red," Dusty introduced. "This's Miss Freddie Wood, she's Mayor of Mulroony. Freddie, this's my cousin, Red Blaze."

"Right pleased, ma'am," Red said, nodding. "Call up your boy, Waldo, let's take a trail count back there, so's we can do it again if we're a hundred or so different from each other."

Smiling at the old joke, Burkman signaled to his assistant who rode forward with a notebook and pencil in his hand. Red and Hamish, as the assistant was known, rode off in the direction of the herd and after a moment Freddie excused herself to Dusty and Burkman and followed.

"I'd like to watch," she said. "Dusty told me about taking a trail count and I would so like to see it done."

"Feel free, ma'am," Red replied, reaching into his hip pocket and producing a couple of lengths of string. He offered one to Freddie, "Here, try your hand at it instead of just sitting."

"It's no' difficult, ma'am," Hamish went on. "Count the legs and divide by four."

"I'll serve you *Irish* whiskey if you try that on me," Freddie warned with a grin.

"I'll be good, ma'am," promised Hamish. "Irish whiskey! Ugh!"

However on reaching a point some hundred yards from the advancing herd, the two men became serious. They halted their horses facing each other and some thirty yards apart, Red holding his cord and with Freddie at his side and Waldo resting the notebook on his saddle before him. On a signal from Red the trail hands started to thin down the herd and soon the cattle began to trickle between the counters. As the cattle went by, Red, Freddie and Hamish counted them and on each hundredth head Red and Freddie made a quick knot in their cord while Hamish put a stroke with his pencil on the paper of his book. Not only did the assistant have to count the cattle, he also watched the animals as they went by, reading the extra-large O.D. Connected road brand burned on each one's left shoulder where it could easily be seen.

Time went by, cattle passed between the counters, cowhands flashed interested and admiring glances at Freddie in passing. At last the drag of the herd went through and the counters came together, each one adding up his or her total.

"How about it, Miss Freddie?" asked Red.

"That's hardly fair," she answered. "It's my first time."

"Make a stab at it anyhow."

"Three thousand, four hundred and fifty-nine head."

Freddie saw the startled manner in which Red and Hamish looked first at her then stared at each other and knew she must have come close to the correct number.

"I get it the same," Red said admiringly.

"And me," Hamish confirmed, his voice tinged with awe. "If you haven't made a trail count before, Miss Freddie, I'll drink that Irish whiskey."

"Then you'll drink it," she smiled. "Come on, let's tell the others."

"Do you want for us to cut out a few head so you can examine them, Waldo?" Dusty asked when the result of the trail count had been passed on.

"No. I'll chance them all dying off on me during the trip to Chicago," the cattle buyer answered, giving his usual reply, for he knew the cattle would be in good condition. "Head them into the pens, let them water and I'll see about starting to put them on the train."

"I'll tend to it, Dusty," Red said, swinging his claybank around and heading for the herd.

Showing their marvellous riding skill, maybe even showing off a mite too, the cowhands brought down their cattle, cutting the line into groups and feeding them into the stock pens so the animals could drink their fill at the water-troughs before being moved on to the waiting railroad cars ready for shipment to Chicago.

Once the herd had been penned, Dusty, Red and Burkman went along to the bank where the sale of the cattle was finished and the small Texan drew enough money to pay off the hands. On discharging their herd,

the O.D. Connected crew had headed for the Fair Lady
Saloon and filed up to collect their wages. Once they
held the money, the cowhands lost no time in starting to
spend it. First the bathhouse received a swarm of
laughing, shouting, singing and wildly-happy men.
From there a visit to a store to buy new clothes was
followed by a stroll – on horseback – around town and
finally the hands gathered in the Fair Lady to celebrate
until, as the Texans put it, the last dog was shot and all
the pups hung.

In all her life Freddie had never seen men buckle
down to enjoying themselves as did the cowhands; and
Dusty was in the thick of everything. He seemed to be
everywhere and wherever he went the laughter and fun
rolled at its highest. Watching Dusty, Freddie realized
why those men, most of them bigger and some maybe
even stronger than him, admired the small Texan and
gave him their loyalty.

It was an exhausting time for the saloongirls. Almost
every girl found herself out on the dance floor and
whirling with cowhands who appeared to possess an
inexhaustible source of energy. Only the four girl band
and the three duty barmaids were not dancing, which
did not mean they relaxed and let the others do all the
work. All were fully occupied with quenching Texas
thirsts and soothing Texas breasts with, if not sweet at
least loud and lively, music.

Then it happened!

"Yeeagh!"

The wild rebel yell rang out and one of the cowhands
drew his Army Colt. A sudden hush that could almost
be felt dropped on the room. All the men knew this
young cowhand. In the war he had ridden in Dusty's
company of the Texas Light Cavalry and proved himself
a brave, if somewhat reckless fighting man. Since then
he had become a tophand with cattle – but he was
dangerous when wet. In other words, when he carried a

load of Old Stump Blaster, he could turn from friendly to mean.

"Yahoo!" he whooped, looking up at the crystal chandelier in the center of the room. "Just watch me bust that fancy doad there."

Slowly Dusty eased back his chair and prepared to rise. Maybe, only maybe, he could prevent Bucky from throwing lead into the chandelier without having to put a bullet into him. Dusty aimed to try. Before he could rise from the table he shared with the civic dignitaries, Dusty felt a hand on his sleeve and turned to meet Freddie's eyes.

"Let me try," she said and rose, crossing the room to where Bucky had a clear space to himself. "I bet I could hit that," she told the young cowhand.

Whatever his faults when drinking, Bucky always respected women. A grin came to his face and he reversed the Colt, offering it to Freddie.

"Take first whirl then, ma'am," he said.

"You're a smart one, trying to get me to take a gun that's not proved empty," Freddie replied. "Only I know about not doing it."

Bucky threw back his head and laughed. "Ma'am, you sure know guns. Want for me to unload the gun?"

"Let's see you shoot first," she answered. "Not the chandelier though, I bet anybody could hit that. How about those decorations on the far wall there?"

Turning on his high heels, Bucky looked across the room and studied the decoration to which Freddie pointed. It was in the shape of the four aces of a deck of cards and about thirty yards away. Every eye in the saloon stayed on Bucky and Freddie, but at his table Dusty grinned and relaxed. The main danger had passed once Freddie started Bucky talking.

"That's a fair target," Bucky drawled, nodding gravely.

"Then how about you showing me how to hit the ace

of clubs first?" Freddie challenged.

Bringing up his Colt, Bucky fired a fast shot that came within three inches of the ace of clubs. He grunted in annoyance and fired again, this time the bullet made a hole a couple of inches off the other side. Twice more Bucky fired, his bullets framing the card and his annoyance growing. Scowling in concentration, he lined his Colt once more. A tension filled the room and the cowhands knew Bucky's temper would explode into violence if he missed again. The gun roared and a hole appeared in the center of the ace of clubs.

At his table Dusty slid the left-side Colt back into its holster and hoped that Bucky did not notice a second hole which had appeared at the same moment as the ace-hitting shot, but a good foot or two above the decoration.

"Yippee!" Freddie whooped and her girls added their shrill yelps of delight to her shout. "It took a real good shot to surround that card, then put one smack in the middle. This calls for a drink, Bucky! Hey, Sarah! Pour out one of your specials for this gentleman."

Without showing any expression at all, Sarah poured out a shot of whisky from one of the top-price bottles. Then, with a deft and practised move, she dropped a small tablet into the drink and shook the glass gently. By the time Bucky had teetered over to the bar there was no sign of the tablet in the drink. Taking the glass, Bucky turned and grinned at Freddie.

"Just watch me when I've drunk this, ma'am," he told her gravely. "I'll be set to show you some real shooting then."

"I just bet you will," she agreed. "Bottoms up, as we say back home."

Tipping up the glass, Bucky sent its contents gliding down his throat to join the other drinks he had taken. Within five seconds of finishing the drink, Bucky forgot his desire to show off his shooting skill. All he wanted to do was sit down; and, on sitting, placed his arms on the table top, rested his head upon them and went peacefully to sleep.

"What happened?" asked Dusty as Freddie returned to their table.

"Bucky wants to go to sleep."

"That I can see."

"It's nothing harmful, although I wouldn't want his head in the morning and he won't feel like eating or drinking much tomorrow."

"And you reckon you need me as town marshal," Dusty grinned.

"And I do. I want to run a saloon, not spend my time going around town pacifying young cowhands who have taken too much drink – Don't you raise your eyebrows at me, Dusty Fog. I don't mind how much they drink as long as they don't want to damage my chandelier."

"Yes'm," Dusty answered, neither looking nor sounding contrite. "You've got a real good point there. Now go entertain your other guests."

From then on the celebration passed by without anything dangerous like incidents involving firearms. The trail crew were in town to celebrate and the O.D. Connected boasted it never did anything by halves. At half past one Freddie made her one mistake of the evening. After watching the hoe-downs and square dances, she insisted on teaching the crowd the *Sir Roger de Coverley*. Her brand knew the tune and Freddie lined up her dancers in two columns, even getting Dusty out on the floor despite his aversion to dancing. The lively and merry tune, calling for frequent changes of part-ners, appealed to cowhand tastes, but was easier started than stopped. Seeing that they must eventually wind up dancing with every girl in the room, the cowhands deter-mined to make sure that they did. Dusty pulled out after a quarter of an hour and leaned on the bar, grinning as he watched Freddie partner first Jimmo, the old ranch cook, then Kiowa, a lean, Indian-dark man who shared the herd's scouting duties with the Kid. Neither were what one could term accomplished dancers, but they made up in gusto what they lacked in grace and poise.

Never had Freddie seen such dancing, it made the sessions at some top hunt's ball pale into insignificance. Not until long after three did the dance end and a dishevelled, exhausted Freddie stated that she was licked and her girls needed their rest. The cowhands raised their objections, but not even the most eager of them felt like carrying on that night. So they piled out of the saloon, carrying along Bucky and such others as had fallen by the wayside. Mounting their horses, the whooping cowhands headed out of town to where their wagons waited. It would be few if any of the crew who spread their bed rolls that night.

Freddie and Dusty stood at the door of the saloon and watched the cowhands depart, then turned to look at the disordered saloon. Girls drooped in their chairs or limped upstairs to bed, tired but happy.

"Whew!" Freddie gasped.

"It'll be like this most nights in the season," Dusty warned.

"I know. Come up to my room and we'll share a pot of coffee. Did you see Shad Birnbaum and Vic Coutland dancing? I can die happy now I've seen that. Oooh! The way my feet feel, I'll die all right. Did you ever try dancing with Jimmo, or Kiowa, Dusty?"

"Can't say I ever did," Dusty admitted. "Fact being I'd rather dance with gals, happen some awkward cuss makes me dance."

Freddie poked her tongue out at him and laughed. "So would I – after tonight. I thought Jimmo was bad enough, but Kiowa—"

"I know. He dances like he was making medicine before taking out after the paleface brother's scalp."

Taking Freddie's arm, Dusty escorted her across the room and upstairs. They went to the main door of Freddie's suite and she opened it. Inside they found Babsy and Waco waiting, although the two youngsters had managed to make themselves comfortable and contrived to keep themselves amused.

"I brought you some coffee up, Miss Freddie," Babsy said, bouncing off Waco's knee. "Is there anything else tonight?"

"Pour out four cups," Freddie replied. "How did you enjoy tonight, Babsy?"

"Cooer, it was ever so good. These Texans don't half go to town when they start, don't they."

"They certainly do," smiled Freddie, watching her maid pour out the coffee. "By the way, Dusty, I had two camp beds put up in Mark's room. I thought you'd like to stay in town, especially as your horses are in the livery barn."

"Shucks, ma'am," Waco grinned. "You'll have to force us hard to accept. I surely loves using the ground for a mattress and the sky for a roof, especially when it's raining."

"Or when there's a good high wind blowing," Dusty agreed. "Thanks, Freddie."

"Don't thank me. I'm merely making sure you don't get a chance to think twice about your offer and get away."

"That's what I like about you, Freddie," Dusty told her, taking his coffee cup. "You're all heart."

"I know, I know. By the way, the town council meets at half past one this afternoon – if they've recovered by that time."

"I'll be along to see them," Dusty promised.

After drinking their coffee and eating a few of the cookies Babsy had fetched from the saloon's kitchen, Dusty and Waco said their good-nights and left the two girls. Mark was asleep when the other two entered his room and they undressed without waking him. Not until the lights were out and they lay in their camp beds did Waco speak.

"What's Miss Freddie mean about the town council meeting, Dusty?"

"You'll find out comes morning, boy."

"That starts to sound like work to me," the youngster groaned.

"You could be right at that, boy," Dusty replied. "Good-night."

"When for?" asked Waco. "Last night or tonight when it comes?"

CHAPTER SIX

I'll Run Your Town — On My Terms

An indignant Mark Counter woke his two friends at ten o'clock in the morning. The blond giant had heard the noise of the celebration the previous night and felt considerably annoyed at having missed it. However the town doctor had ordered that Mark stayed in bed for forty-eight hours and Miss Freddie Woods proved strong-willed enough to see he did.

"Hid my clothes she has," Mark told his two *amigos* in an aggrieved tone. "Is she any kin of yours, Dusty?"

"I sure hope not," Dusty grinned.

At the moment a knock sounded at the door and one of Freddie's swampers entered carrying a bucket of hot water.

"Figured you gents'd be waking about now," he remarked. "Man, that was some whing-ding last night."

"How'd you like hanging feet first out of the window?" Mark growled.

"Ignore him, friend," Waco told the startled swamper. "He's just all mean-mouthed and ornery 'cause he done slept through the fun last night."

"There'll be two of you hanging out of that window in a minute, boy!" Mark warned. "Dusty, can't you keep these hired hands of yours under control in a sick man's room?"

"Shucks, the boy's too young and this gent's too old

and set in his ways,'' Dusty answered. "Is Miss Freddie awake yet?''

"Nope," grinned the swamper. "Nor any of her girls 'cepting Big Sarah and even she looks a mite peaked.''

However by the time Dusty and Waco had washed and dressed, they found Freddie had crawled from bed. After eating breakfast in Mark's room, and describing the fun much to the blond giant's annoyance, Freddie went downstairs to check her bar stocks while Dusty and Waco headed for the livery barn and collected their horses. On reaching the O. D. Connected camp, Dusty found most of the men awake and received apologies from a slightly green-looking Bucky for any trouble the young man might have caused the previous night.

"Morning, Cousin Dusty," Red greeted, coming forward with a plate of food in his hands; a sight which caused Bucky's hurried departure. "Now that was what I call a night.''

"It sure was," Dusty agreed. "Look out there, Cousin Red. Seems like folks took my warning to heart.''

Already a second herd of cattle was approaching the town and behind it, at varying distances stretching back to the far horizon were three more.

"I've looked," Red replied and grinned. "Make that first one to be Uncle Charlie's. We sure wiped his eye, getting here ahead of him.''

"That'll please Uncle Devil," Dusty answered, also grinning. "I'll grab me a shave, then we'll ride over and see Uncle Charlie. Or don't you want to come?''

"I wouldn't miss it. I sure want to see Uncle Charlie's face and hear what he has to say when he finds that you and I licked him here.''

"Not me, Red. It's your drive and has been since the start.''

Colonel Charles Goodnight, master trail boss and man whose early findings made the great inter-State cattle drives possible, studied his two young nephews and heard their news in silence that was as ominous as the calm before a storm. At last the silence broke and he let flow a blistering string of the most lurid oaths either Dusty or Red could ever remember hearing; except when something riled their Uncle Devil. At the end of his tirade, Goodnight bellowed with laughter, slapped Red on the shoulder and commended him on a damned good job well done.

"I got your word about Brownton, Dustine," Goodnight went on. "Was fixed to go there myself, but I changed my mind when I heard about that damnable no-guns for Texans rule. Say, where's your herd?"

"Shipped out already," Dusty replied. "The pens are empty and you can go straight on in. Waldo Burkman's in town."

"He'll be waiting for me, I shouldn't wonder," Goodnight grunted. "I'll go tend to my herd. See you boys in town."

"We'll be around, sir," Dusty promised and watched his uncle ride away. Turning to Red, Dusty went on, "I've got to be in town before half past one."

"Business or pleasure?"

"Business first. Freddie wants me to handle the law until Kail Beauregard can get up here."

"Does huh?" Red grunted. "Reckon you'll need me here?"

"I could use you, but somebody has to take the cattle-drive money home to Uncle Devil—"

"And explain to him where you bunch are."

"That too," Dusty grinned.

"Was talking to Jimmo afore you came out, Dusty. He reckons another day'll see him ready for heading home. So's Kiowa and most of the boys."

"It's your choice," Dusty replied. "Come on, I want to send Kiowa and Waco out to learn who owns the other drives that are coming in. I sure hope it isn't Clay Allison just yet."

Not until two o'clock did the final member of the

Mulrooney town council enter the dining room of Freddie's suite at the Fair Lady. Coutland entered and took his place at the long table. Like all the others, he looked a mite dark under the eyes and showed signs of feeling the effects of the previous night's revelry.

"Sorry I'm late," he said.

"None of us were early," Freddie answered. "Now gentlemen, to business. It would appear that our town is drawing the trail drive trade. Not only has Colonel Goodnight's herd entered the stock pens, but Shanghai Pierce, Waxachie Smith and George Littlefield's herds are coming in. They are all big ranchers and have crews of over twenty men each. Not only that, but I have met one of the top buffalo hide buyers and he has passed word out that he is making his rendezvous here. To cap it all, the railroad men have heard about our town's little party last night and are regarding us with interest."

"Then we're made," Birnbaum put in, looking unhappy at having nothing to worry him.

"Not exactly, Shad, there is one slight problem."

"What's that, Miss Freddie?" Dongedon asked, thinking of the trade his saloon had garnered the previous night.

"Law enforcement. The railroad won't build out of a wild, wide-open town."

"And what might your solution be, Freddie?" Coutland asked. "We know you have one."

"I wish to hire an Indian Nations lawman called Kail Beauregard."

"I've never heard of him," Coutland said and looked at the other men but none of them admitted to knowing the name. "Why not try to hire Earp, or Hickok?"

"Because I want to hire a man who can handle cowhands without using a gun or cracking skulls. Besides, men like Earp or Hickok invite trouble by bringing in show-offs and would-be fast guns to try their skill. Captain Fog recommended Kail Beauregard to me."

"If that's the case, I'm for Beauregard," one of the

council stated and a rumble of agreement went up among the others.

"We'll vote it formally," Freddie stated. "All in favor of hiring Kail Beauregard, signify by raising the right hand."

The vote was unanimous and Coutland asked, "How soon can we get him here?"

"In four – five weeks," Freddie replied.

"Then how—?"

"Captain Fog agreed to pinch-hit for Beauregard until he arrives."

Once more the eager and excited talk rumbled up. At last Birnbaum managed to make himself heard over the others and asked, "How much will Captain Fog want paying for this, Miss Freddie?"

"We didn't discuss it. He's waiting outside, may I ask him in?"

"Of course," Coutland replied.

Dusty entered the room, conscious that every eye was on him. Crossing to the table, he took his seat and looked at the circle of faces.

"We want you to handle the law for us, Captain Fog," Coutland said. "If you accept, we're prepared to offer you one hundred dollars a month and seventy-five for your deputies, plus a twenty-five per cent bonus taken from all fines."

"That's a fair offer," Dusty answered. "But I'm not taking it. I'll be here for four weeks and I want one hundred and twenty-five dollars for me, one hundred for each deputy – but the fine money goes entirely to the town."

"That could lose you money, Dusty," Freddie objected.

"Likely. But I've never liked this sharing in the fine money idea. It makes some lawmen go grabbing everybody they can lay their hands on, just for extra money. That builds up a dislike for the lawmen. I'd sooner folks knew I was arresting them for doing something wrong, not that I'm grabbing a chance to put more money into my pocket.''

''You've a good thought there, Captain,'' Coutland remarked. ''It never struck me in that light before.''

''There's another thing I want straight right now. If I'm hired I'll run your town – on my terms.''

''And they are?'' asked Freddie.

''First, I alone hire the deputies, I don't get asked by *anybody* to take on an out-of-work nephew, brother-in-law or cousin. Policing a town like this one will become hard enough without untrained help to watch over.''

''That's reasonable,'' grunted one of the men.

''Second, I want a civic ordinance empowering me to inspect, or have inspected, every gambling device in town, any time I feel like it.''

''Are you saying Miss Freddie and I run dishonest games?'' Dongelon growled.

''There'll be a lot more than you and Freddie running games in town soon,'' Dusty answered. ''Some of them won't be honest and I want the legal right to inspect them without wasting time with a warrant.''

''That's reasonable, Dongelon,'' Coutland remarked.

''I agree, and back the motion,'' the burly saloon-keeper replied. ''The house percentage satisfies me without needing any more of an edge.''

''How many deputies are you going to need, Captain?'' asked Birnbaum.

''Mark, the Kid, Waco, one more – and Big Sarah.''

''Big Sarah?'' Freddie gasped.

''I don't want her full-time. But there'll be times when I have to get a woman searched, which same me and the boys can't do. So I want a woman deputy and one who can take care of herself.''

''Sarah can do that all right,'' Freddie admitted. ''I'll ask her if she'll accept the offer.''

''And I figure to make each trail boss an honorary deputy marshal responsible for the good behavior of his men. Which same applies to the railroad, I'll want one of their gang bosses; and to the hide buyers. You can either make some small payment to the men, or arrange some privilege to go with the badge."

"That's easy enough arranged," Coutland agreed.

"*Bueno*," Dusty drawled. "Did Miss Freddie tell you what armament I want at the office?"

"Not yet, Dusty, but I'll do it now."

Quickly Freddie told the council of Dusty's suggestions and his reasons for wanting the various arms. The men agreed to purchase half-a-dozen shotguns and a Sharps Old Reliable rifle without arguing about their cost. Then Birnbaum made what, to his Eastern-trained mind, was an obvious suggestion.

"Why not make everybody in town hand all their firearms over to the marshal and only collect them when they need them?"

"No!" The one word popped out of Dusty's mouth like the crack of a black-snake whip.

"It sounds reasonable to me," one of the other men remarked.

"It doesn't to me," Coutland objected. "I've a shotgun at home and I like to use it for hunting. Would I have to draw it out when I decide to go and hand it in on my return?"

"There could be exceptions—" Birnbaum began.

"No there couldn't," Dusty interrupted, "or you'd wind up just like Brownton tried to be."

"But your work would be easier and safer if nobody but your men had guns," one of the storekeepers pointed out.

"Sure would – if *nobody* but us had guns," Dusty agreed. "Trouble with that being that only the honest, law-abiding citizens would turn in their guns. Or do you reckon an outlaw would be so scared of breaking a civic ordinance by owning a gun that he'd give it up?"

"If you put it that way—"

"I do. Disarm the honest man and you put him at the mercy of the armed outlaw. Take Mr. Birnbaum's idea of folks only drawing out the gun when you need it. That's swell, only I can't see an owlhoot who's sticking your place up letting you trot down to the marshal's office to draw out your gun so you can defend your property. Now can any of you see it?''

The idea of an armed outlaw permitting his victim to go collect a gun and awaiting his return amused the members of the council, but it also showed them the futility and stupidity of Birnbaum's suggestion.

''You've made your point, Dusty,'' Freddie smiled. ''But how do we avoid having shootings in town?''

''There's no real way you can. But happen two men aim to fight, they'll do it with or without guns. You can avoid a lot of wild shooting though. Put aside a place where the fellers can shoot off their guns without endangering the town. Or have some targets set up in a safe place in the saloon, like Freddie has. And give the trail hands a fair deal, don't cheat them blind like most Kansas towns do. That way they'll not have a resentment against you and want to show you how good they are with a gun.''

''But how about armed robberies?'' Coutland asked.

''Make it known that armed robbery, with a gun or a knife, will be classed as done with intent to murder and see the judge goes the limit in punishing any offenders. That's what I reckon's the best answer.''

''We'll see to that for you,'' Freddie promised.

''And if there's a complaint laid against a visitor, make sure it's investigated from both sides, not just from the local businessmen's angle.''

''We'll let you do that,'' Coutland promised.

''Then you've got yourself some law,'' Dusty drawled.

''I don't think we'll regret having it,'' Birnbaum stated. ''Hey, Captain. I have a gun under my store counter but I'm not good with it. Would you teach me how to handle it?''

"Glad to. There's one thing you want to do with it for a start though."

"What's that?"

"Put it away until you know how to handle it properly. An untrained man with a gun is more dangerous to himself and his friends than to his enemies."

"By cracky," grinned one of the men. "I believe you're right."

"I *know* I'm right," Dusty replied but he was not smiling. "Well, I'll go collect Waco and we'll make a start."

Rising, Dusty left the room. For a time none of the Mulrooney town council spoke. Then Coutland slapped the table top with his big hand and gave a bellow of laughter.

"By George!" he boomed. "I'll bet we get that spur line through here after all. Don't you, Freddie?"

"For the first time in days I feel we've a better than even chance," she replied. "And now let's make a start at doing the things Du – Captain Fog requested. Somehow I don't think he's a young man who would be pleased with any delay."

Dusty found Waco waiting for him in the barroom. Leaving Babsy at the table where he had been entertaining the girl, Watco walked forward.

"How'd it go, Dusty?" he asked.

"We're lawmen, boy."

"Never been one afore. Do we get us badges and all?"

"And all," agreed Dusty. "Only there's more to being a lawman than just wearing a badge and walking the rounds. Let's go along to the jail and I'll tell you as much as I can about it."

Accompanied by wild cowhand yells, the Goodnight J.A. crew came thundering along Main Street as Dusty and Waco walked towards the marshal's office. Dusty halted and Waco stopped at his side, standing watching a familiar scene and one in which Waco played a prominent role the previous day as the O.D. Connected arrived in town. On reaching the Fair Lady, the J.A. crew left their horses at the hitching rail and headed inside to wait until Goodnight came and paid them off.

"Tonight's going to be lively, boy," Dusty remarked and entered the office.

And lively it proved to be. There were five crews in town and both saloons drew a large and lusty mixed trade as railroad construction workers arrived by the evening work train. For the first time in his life Waco found himself on the other side of the lawman fence, although he did not work alone. He also saw the swift, efficient and effective manner in which Dusty dealt with trouble. Not that they had any real trouble that night. A few fist fights, a couple of cowhands shooting off their guns on the street and several rowdy drunks being all that emerged. Some fifteen assorted celebrators wound up in jail; not that it meant much for they would be released on payment of a fine the following morning.

The Kid rode in at midnight, arriving at the jail with news that he had made a big circle and Billy Jack was still out. Between them, the two men had given warning of Brownton's laws and ways to several herds and arranged to have the information passed back down trail. Then he put up his horse at the livery barn and after a meal went to sleep in the deputies' night room at the jail. Dusty felt easier knowing the Kid was on hand ready to help out. Not that Dusty mistrusted Waco, but the youngster had a lot to learn about being a lawman.

Not until four in the morning did Dusty and Waco manage to get off their feet. Instead of riding out to the O.D. Connected trail camp or using the beds at the Fair Lady, they went to the office's sleeping quarters. The prisoners in the cells were all asleep and the two Texans sat on their beds removing their boots. Waco worked his toes and groaned.

"What's wrong, boy?" Dusty asked.

"I never knowed being a lawman was so hard on the feet," Waco answered wryly. "I tell you, Dusty, walking's only good when you're doing it on the back of a horse."

"Sure," Dusty agreed. "And this's easy, boy. We only had two *honest* saloons and a handful of decent folk to deal with tonight. You wait a spell, maybe for two days, until that Brownton pack learn the way things are going. Then we'll be seeing a real prime selection of sharks flocking in here looking for easy pickings."

"Which same'll likely mean more walking for me?"

"That's just about what it means, boy."

Until a very few weeks back any man who had dared call Waco "boy" would have wound up with a fight on his hands. Even now the youngster would accept the name only from Dusty, Mark, the Kid and Red Blaze. Way Waco saw it, those four were his *amigos* and as close as any brothers; anyway, the way they said it, they figured he would one day grow up into a real good *man*.

Not that Waco thought of Dusty's use of the word "boy", his feelings being more on the aching condition of his feet. Cowhand boots had never been designed for excessive amounts of walking and he sure did not want a whole slew of footwork in the future if he could avoid it.

"Isn't there any way we can stop the sharks getting in?" Waco asked.

"I'm thinking about just that, boy," Dusty replied.

CHAPTER SEVEN

Dusty's Welcome Mat

No incident of note marked Dusty's second day in office as marshal of Mulrooney. He sent a telegraph to the county sheriff's office and received a reply appointing him and his men special sheriff's deputies; a shrewd move which gave him and his men the legal right to act outside the city limits and within the county's boundaries – which included Brownton, although Dusty had not thought about the matter. The shotguns, Sharps rifle and ammunition arrived and one of Freddie's swampers proved to Dusty's satisfaction that he would make a suitable jailer. Although at first Big Sarah was inclined to treat her appointment as deputy in the nature of a joke, she soon changed her mind. Along with Dusty, the Kid and Mark – the latter newly from his bed and with his left arm in a sling – Sarah took the oath of office and pinned a badge on her dress. Then Dusty told her the extent of her duties. At the end of his instructions, Sarah no longer regarded the business as a joke.

Three Brownton citizens visited Mulrooney during the day and looked around them with considerable interest. They came independently and returned to Brownton to report their findings to their respective employers. The news brought by the trio spread gloom and despondency amongst those who hoped that Brownton would become a new trail drive Mecca, end of the long pilgrimage from Texas. One of the employers had expected nothing more since witnessing the departure of first Dusty Fog and then the cattle buyers; and so decided to put into operation a plan begun the day of Brownton's idiocy. Other citizens of Brownton gave consideration to the situation and the results of one school of thought showed when the eastbound train pulled out at noon the following day.

The eastbound train came slowly to a halt at Mulrooney's depot and began to disgorge its passengers, although there appeared to be some delay as the conductor checked on tickets.

A tall, elegantly dressed man and a beautiful stylishly attired young woman were the first to leave the train. Standing on the depot platform, they looked around and the man nodded. Placing her dainty little parasol on her shoulder, the girl took the man's arm and they started to walk forward. They did not get far.

"The train pulls out in fifteen minutes," Dusty Fog said, stepping from the agent's office and blocking the couple's path. "Don't go too far from here."

"Why?" asked the man, scowling down at the new marshal's badge on Dusty's calf-skin vest.

"You're leaving with it."

For a moment the man did not speak, then he grinned knowingly, winked at Dusty and reached into his inside breast pocket.

"All right," he began, "how mu—?"

Which was as far as he got. Dusty came forward with a gliding step and whipped around his right hand, driving his bunched fist full into the pit of the man's stomach. Giving a croak of agony which testified to the force behind the blow, the man clutched at his middle and folded over, dropping to his knees.

"Don't try it!" Dusty warned as the girl brought her parasol from her shoulder.

"You just lay a hand on me!" she screeched in reply.

"Lady, I wouldn't touch you with a long fishing

pole," Dusty answered and raised his voice. "Miss Sarah!"

Once more the office door opened and Big Sarah stepped out. It was not the jovial, rouged and made-up Big Sarah who served behind the Fair Lady's bar, but a well-scrubbed, grim-faced woman wearing a dark suit and with a deputy's badge on her jacket's left lapel. Taking in the scene with a quick glance, Big Sarah advanced to Dusty's side and faced the girl.

"Try using that spoke on me, girlie," she warned, "and I'll make you eat it."

One quick-taken glance told the girl that Big Sarah could most likely do it too. So she lowered the sharp-pointed parasol, which had taken a miner's eye out in Quiet Town, and bent over her groaning escort. The man looked up at Dusty with agony twisting his face.

"Th – there was no call for that," he croaked, hoping to gain sympathy from the watching crowd.

"I figured you might be pulling a gun," Dusty answered.

"G – gun! I was reaching for my wallet."

"That'd be called attempted bribery in a lot of places. The judge here's real strong on attempted bribery they do say," Dusty countered. "Want me to push it to him?"

"No – no. I'll get out of here."

"Thought you'd come round to seeing it my way," drawled Dusty.

Catching sight of another familiar face from his days in Quiet Town, Dusty turned and walked away with Big Sarah at his side. The man dragged himself slowly and painfully to his feet, then gave a low snarl and his right hand went towards the cuff on his left sleeve. Shooting out her hand, the girl caught her escort's sleeve and nodded to his left. Turning, the man looked in the indicated direction and what he saw sent a chilly sensation running through him. Waco stood with his shoulder against a stack of freight boxes, the deputy's badge prominent on his calf-skin vest and his right hand thumb-hooked into his belt not more than a couple of inches from the walnut grips of his off-side Colt.

Giving a shrug, the man – he was a crooked gambler who used the girl as a steerer and lure to attract gullible victims – forgot his intentions. Usually a trail-end town such as Mulrooney offered good pickings, especially in its early days before things became too organized. If his reception went to prove anything, Mulrooney appeared to have organized fast and there would be no chance of his settling down in the town. Taking the girl's arm, the man went back to the train and climbed aboard. Not until the danger to Dusty had passed did Waco relax or move. The youngster was learning fast and already knew how to cover his partner as a good lawman should.

As she walked along at Dusty's side, Big Sarah looked at the people in front of the train and wondered which of them attracted Dusty's attention. Then a frown creased her face as she saw they were making for a tall, slim man wearing the low crowned black Stetson, black cutaway jacket, white broadcloth shirt and string bow-tie, fancy vest and striped pants of a professional gambler. Although the man dressed well and wore an ivory butted Army Colt in a fast draw holster, Sarah did not consider him to be the kind they had come to the depot to prevent entering town. She need not have worried. On seeing Dusty approaching, the man's face broke into a warm smile and he held out his hand.

"Howdy, Dusty," he said.

"Howdy, Frank," Dusty replied, knowing Frank Derringer to be an honest gambler and being particularly pleased to see the man. "I'd like to see you at the office when you've settled in."

"That sounds ominous," Derringer answered, still smiling.

"You don't know the half of it. Anybody interesting on the train?"

"Ludlow and Bessie, but you already saw them. A few others you'd likely remember if they get off – which I don't think they will, and – hey now, there comes the cream of the bunch. That fat guy in the check suit and derby and the lean, hatcheted faced cuss who're getting down at the far end of the smoker car. They work with a rauchy little cuss who looks like he'd jump a mile high if a door banged behind him. I saw that little cuss kill two men on Newton."

Turning, Dusty glanced to where the men in question had left the train. Then Dusty caught Mark Counter's eye and nodded to the two men. Mark nodded and moved forward to block the two men's path.

"Don't go too far, gents," he warned. "The train pulls out real soon."

The fat man studied Mark's big frame, taking in the left arm in its sling, the matched, low hanging guns and finally Mark's deputy badge. Then he raised his eyes to study Mark's face and his expression was one of polite, innocent interest as he beamed and said:

"I fail to catch the drift of your remark, my good minion of the law, my friend and I are but traveling salesmen—"

"Then you've run into bad luck," Mark interrupted. "This town's got more than enough of what you're selling."

"Now see here, young man," boomed the fat tinhorn indignantly. "The mayor of your town happens to be a personal friend of mine. He and I went to college together I'll have you know."

"He's a she, and real choosey about her friends. Be on the train when it pulls out, mister, you'll find it's safer."

While the fat man had been holding Mark's attention, his pard moved around to approach the big Texan from Mark's left side. Way the hatchet-faced man saw it, the big deputy couldn't do much with his left arm and ought to be easy meat. With that thought in mind, the man started to raise his right fist.

"Hey!" a voice behind him said.

Hatchet-face turned; which proved to be one hell of a
mistake. The Ysabel Kid had come up unnoticed behind
him and brought around the old "yellow boy", driving
its brass-shod butt plate against the man's jaw in a blow
that would have gladdened the heart of a bayonet-
fighting instructor had one seen it. Landing with some
power, the blow sprawled Hatchet-Face to one side and
ended his ideas of attacking Mark from the rear.

"See here n—!" began the fat man.

The cause of his stopping the indignant tirade which
rose in his throat was that same throat being gripped by
something which felt like the steel jaws of a bear trap,
but was in reality only Mark's good right hand. After
shaking the man, Mark gave him a heave that staggered
him towards the train where he landed almost at the feet
of a small, mild-looking jasper in a cheap city suit and
who looked two shades more timid than a well-hunted
whitetail deer. Looking down, the small man's lips
tightened and his right fingers moved towards his
jacket. Then he stopped and glanced around the area,
seeing not two but, if he counted Big Sarah, five peace
officers present. Being a wise man, he decided to
overlook the mishandling of his two junior partners and
also to find a town which offered more scope for his
particular brand of game of chance. In this he showed
more wisdom than he knew; while his appearance had
lulled more than one man's suspicions until too late, this
time he was known. If he had attempted to draw the
little Smith and Wesson revolver from under his jacket,
Dusty would have killed him; for some word of this
trio's activities had reached the small Texan. Dusty had
prevented the man entering his town, thanks to Frank
Derringer's warning.

Several people who left Brownton with the intention
of settling down in the greener pastures of Mulrooney

had watched the spreading of Dusty's welcome mat and the way the local law jerked it from under the feet of the unwelcome; and changed their minds, staying on the train with the intention of seeking a more friendly kind of town.

One woman did not take the hint or give so much as a glance at the discomforted deportees. Climbing out of the smoker, she stood with firm-planted feet and looked around her. She was as big as Big Sarah and maybe a few pounds heavier, which made her a tolerable piece of woman-flesh in one lump. Yet, like Sarah, there appeared to be little flabby fat on her body. She wore a stylish mauve traveling outfit, a large brimmed, fancy hat and sported some good jewelery. Under its makeup her face seemed to be jovial and not bad looking. Twirling her vanity bag, she glanced at the porter who lifted a couple of bags from the train and told him to set them down, handing him a dollar piece.

"Howdy, ma'am," Dusty greeted, walking up to the woman. "I'd like to see you in the depot agent's office."

A frown creased the woman's brow as she studied Dusty's badge. Then she gave a philosophical shrug and followed Dusty into the office, Big Sarah watched them go before joining Mark, the Kid and Waco.

"Cap'n Fog's welcome mat sure works," she grinned. "I saw two tinhorns on the train, real mean cusses. They're still aboard."

"It's all done by kindness and setting an example, Sarah," Mark grinned. "Who was the lady Dusty took into the office?"

"That was no lady, that was Lily Gouch, she ran a cathouse in Newton."

"Reckon she allows to run one here," the Kid remarked. "There isn't one and no town should be without a house."

"You're polite with it," Lily Grouch remarked for

Dusty had held open the office door to let her enter. "Fast but polite."

"With what, ma'am?" Dusty replied.

"Don't play games," the woman growled, opening her vanity bag. "How much now and how much a week?"

"I hope that doesn't mean what I'm sure it means."

The voice came from the door of the inner office. Giving a muttered exclamation, Lily turned and looked in the direction of the speaker. So did Dusty, for he had no idea that Freddie Woods had decided to come and view his welcome mat in operation. Clearly she had, for the lady mayor of Mulrooney came into the room and closed the door behind her.

"Who're you?" Lily asked, studying Freddie's expensive clothes and elegant appearance.

"My name is Woods, Freddie Woods."

"You're the dame who runs that fancy Fair Lady Saloon?"

"I'm the dame, I'm also mayor of Mulrooney and part of our marshal, Captain Fog's welcome committee. Now you know who we are, how about making it equal by telling us who you are."

"Lily Gouch. Say, you're quick and open. Most towns let me settle in before they send one of their hired help to put the bite on."

"Miss Gouch," Freddie said quietly. "I'm trying hard to like you, give me a little help. There are certain things I want settled—"

"So all right. Tell me how much you want."

"For what?"

"For letting me run a brothel in your nice, clean little town!" Lily answered, her voice rising higher. "That's for what!"

All Lily's grown life had been spent in and around brothels, first as one of the girls and then becoming a madam. In town after town she had paid out her bribe money to stay open and in business; although the name given to her contributions differed from town to town. Some folks called it "campaign funds", others used the term "civic charities", but whatever name it went under Lily knew the money found its way into the pockets of the top-level civic dignitaries.

So all right, a madam grew to expect that kind of incidental expense and adjusted her profit margin to take it into consideration. But it shook even a hardened old hand at the madam business to enter a new town and be met with the demands at the railroad depot before she even bought her house and set up the business. Anger at the injustice of it all made Lily act rashly. Even if her words meant losing a chance of settling in Mulrooney, she aimed to tell those two hypocrites just what she thought of them and their town.

"That's what I said!" she spat out. "I run a brothel. I'm not giving it any fancy names. Does that make you blush, dearie?"

An icy calm dripped from Freddie's voice as she said, "Wait outside, Dusty. There are a few things I want to say to Miss Gouch and I'd rather not embarrass you by saying them in your presence."

While Dusty had considerable faith in Freddie's ability to handle most situations, he thought she might be biting off a sizeable hunk more than she could chew this time. The madam was taller, heavier and, unless he missed his guess, knew a fair slew about rough-house brawling. Not that it figured to come to a brawl for he doubted if Freddie would do such a thing – Dusty had not heard of Freddie's clash with Big Sarah. However, he did not argue but turned on his heel and left the office. Outside, a jerk of his head brought Big Sarah to him.

"Need something, Cap'n?" she asked.

"Maybe. Stand here for a spell. Freddie's in there with Lily Gouch."

"Oh boy!" Sarah grinned. "I hope Lily keeps a civil tongue in her head."

"Get set to go in if the furniture starts breaking," Dusty replied.

"To help Lily? 'Cause the boss doesn't need help. She's a mite slow on the hair-yanking, but she packs a punch in both hands – I know."

Dusty was still not convinced and at any moment expected to hear the sound of a brawl starting. Instead all the sound which emerged through the door appeared to be a rapid, low rumble in Freddie's voice and which formed one of the finest flows of vituperation Dusty could remember hearing in years. A chuckle from his side told Dusty that Big Sarah could also hear Freddie's words.

"I didn't reckon the boss knew half of them," Sarah remarked admiringly. "And I bet Lily Gouch didn't expect 'em either."

After Dusty left the office, Freddie faced the madam and looked her straight in the eye.

"I suppose your mention of the brothel was supposed to make me blush, shriek and run from the room with my hands over my ears," Freddie said. "All right, pin back *your* ears and listen."

With that Freddie proceeded to show off a knowledge of a certain section of the English language not usually associated with ladies of refinement and good breeding. She used the knowledge gained from stable-hands and grooms as a child in England and around British Army camps while visiting various relatives, improved on it with the inspired utterings of sailors and freighters, embellishing the whole with cowhand, buffalo hunter and railroad men's curses and topped the whole boiling with a liberal helping devised by her own active imagination.

At first anger flushed Lily's face, then amazement and finally admiration for the flow of language took its place. Lily reckoned to be a better than fair hand at cursing herself, but admitted that she could not compete with that neatly-dressed dude gal.

"And if you want to make anything more of it,"

Freddie finished, "we'll try rolling on the floor for a time."

Being the madam of a brothel often called for a skill in the art of fisticuffs and did not tend to make a woman meek, mild and defenseless; but Lily decided to decline taking up Freddie's challenge. Lily reckoned that anybody who could curse with such ease must also be better than fair at handling her end in a physical brawl and, while not being scared, she decided to listen to what Miss Freddie Woods had to say.

"Go ahead," she told Freddie. "You've convinced me that you're worth listening to."

"There's not much to say. You want to open and run a place of business and handle a service that I and my girls are not willing to supply to our customers. That suits me fine, I know men want that service and would rather them be able to obtain it freely than have some girl who doesn't want to get raped."

"You talk plain enough, girlie," Lily said. "I'll give you that."

"I think it's best," Freddie answered. "That way we both understand each other. Now you want to open a house in town. When I helped arrange the layout I thought somebody might and had a place that might suit you built. It lies on the opposite side of town to the church and main residential area and in a small grove of trees. I thought that might be best, not everybody agrees with my views on this matter."

"I'll say they don't," breathed Lily, staring in a fascinated manner at Freddie. Never had she met a woman, even a hardened madam, who treated her business in such a frank, matter-of-fact manner.

"If you wish to buy the house, you'll find the price reasonable. You'll be expected to pay the same civic taxes as a comparable business in town."

It never occurred to Lily to doubt Freddie's words or suspect the girl of trying to either make a huge profit or hike up a plushy level of "taxes" which were in reality nothing more or less than bribes.

"I'm still with you, Miss Woods."

"The name's Freddie. One thing I want you to ensure, that you run an orderly house."

"An orderly disorderly house," grinned Lily.

"Just that," Freddie smiled in return. "And I don't want your girls touting for trade on the streets. Apart from that, you're free to run your business the way you wish to run it. There'll be no contributions to charity, campaign funds or any other cause of that kind. I'll promise you that no matter who handles the law in town."

"You know something," Lily said soberly, holding out her hand. "I bet you will at that."

Freddie and Lily left the office on the best of terms and remained friends as long as they stayed in Mulrooney. The big building in the grove became known as the most orderly, well run disorderly house in the United States and there was never any unpleasantness or trouble with Lily's girls.

"Is everything all right, Freddie?" Dusty asked as Lily went to collect her baggage from by the train.

"Fine," Freddie replied, glancing around her and noticing a number of sullen faces peering through the windows on the train. "It looks as if your end went off smoothly, too."

"Why sure," Dusty agreed. "We spread the welcome mat, just like I said we would."

"All set, Cap'n?" asked the conductor, strolling up.

"Sure is, friend."

"I keep 'em held up long enough for you to cut the herd?"

"Yep."

Dusty had expected the arrival of a number of undesirables from Brownton and made arrangements with the conductor of the Eastbound to delay the passengers leaving his train, giving the Mulrooney law time to look over those who left and cull out the undesirables. The conductor had played his part admirably and a number of travelers decided not to bother leaving his train at Mulrooney after all.

Just as the train pulled out, Banker Coutland strolled up. In addition to running the bank, Coutland also operated the town's real estate business. From the delighted beam on his face, he had good news to impart and it was to do with his secondary interest as Freddie's party discovered.

"Hah, Freddie!" he boomed. "Your people told me I'd find you here. I've sold that vacant saloon along the street from your place. It's to a saloon-keeper who was in Brownton but didn't like the way things were going there. I hope you don't mind me letting it go."

"It's your business," Freddie replied. "As long as the new owner is willing to accept our rules, I won't object."

"She seemed satisfied."

"She?" Freddie asked. "Who bought the saloon?"

"Buffalo Kate Gilgore," replied the banker. "She'll be moving down in a couple of days."

The name meant nothing to Freddie – yet.

CHAPTER EIGHT

Waco's Education

"Gent to see you, Dusty," Waco said, entering the marshal's office.

The train had departed, taking with it as ripe a collection of tinhorn gamblers, gold-brick salesmen and assorted petty criminals as might be found anywhere other than in a State or Territorial prison, and Dusty was seated in his private office at the jail.

Rising, Dusty strolled out into the main office and nodded a welcome to Frank Derringer. Going to the main office's desk, Dusty opened its drawer and took out a deputy's badge, dropping it on the desk top before the gambler.

"Pin her on, Frank," he said.

"Me?"

"The boy's name's Waco, none of the rest of us 'cept you are called Frank."

"I'm no lawman, Dusty. My religion is devout coward."

"I reckon you'll do for what I want," Dusty replied, knowing the gambler to have sand to burn when the chips went down. "Anyway, happen there comes danger you can always hide behind Big Sarah. That's what I do."

"And me," Waco grinned. "But don't worry, there's

room for us all, 'cepting Mark's head behind the –
Eeeyow!''

The latter came as Mark and Big Sarah descended on
Waco. One moved in at either side of the youngster
without his realizing how close they were to him.
Although neither of them spoke, each reached out and
took a firm hold of the youngster's ears and led him,
yelping his apologies, through the door and into a cell.

"He looks more natural in there," Big Sarah
remarked, locking the door.

"Sure does," Mark agreed.

"All right, all right," Waco yelled. "I apologize.
There's even room for Mark's head behind you."

"That lets you out with me, boy, but not with
Sarah," Mark grinned.

"I'd best let him out, or I'll have Babsy jumping
me," Sarah went on.

While his deputies let off some of their high spirits,
Dusty went on talking with Derringer. Dusty outlined
his plan to check on all the games in town and his need
for a man with knowledge of a fair number of the tricks
crooked gamblers used to rook their victims. While
Derringer was a completely honest gambler, he needed
to know the crooked tricks to protect his interests. That
Dusty would have need of such specialized knowledge
was apparent to the small Texan from the start and he
had been on the lookout for a straight gambler to take
on as deptuy. Of all the honest gamblers he knew, Dusty
was most pleased to see Frank Derringer and hoped the
man would agree to help out.

"I hoped to get a job dealing for some house in
town," Derringer remarked.

"You can do that too. All I want to do is have you
around when there's a check made on the various
games."

"Danged if I don't give it a whirl," grinned
Derringer. "Slap on the badge and swear me in."

By the time Dusty had sworn in his new deputy, Sarah, Mark and Waco were finished in the cells and returned to the front office. Sarah remarked that she had to go back to the Fair Lady and Mark stated that as he was still all weak and feeble from his wound he aimed to catch some sleep before coming on to help with the evening rounds.

"You're off watch tonight, boy," Dusty said as Sarah, Mark and the Kid left the office.

"Why sure," agreed the youngster cautiously.

"Seeing Babsy?"

"Yep. Miss Freddie gave her the night off and we aim to take us a buggy ride after we've had supper at the hotel."

The friendship between Waco and the volatile little Babsy had been a source of some unexpressed amusement amongst the youngster's *amigos*. It was an innocent enough affair which ebbed and flowed depending on how the mood took either Babsy or Waco at the moment. However this would be the first opportunity the two had had of getting together in an evening, for each other night Waco found himself on watch as Dusty's deputy and Babsy had her work at the Fair Lady to keep her occupied. For all that, when Waco visited the Fair Lady he usually wound up sitting with Babsy and the other girls appeared to respect her prior claim for none of them ever tried to cut in on the handsome young deputy.

"Dangerous things, buggy rides," Dusty stated. "How'd you like to come along with Derry and me to check over the games at the Fair Lady and Dongelon's Wooden Spoon?"

Interest showed on Waco's face. "Gee, I'd like that swell. I don't have to meet Babsy until seven so there's time."

One thing Dusty had learned early about Waco was that the youngster possessed an insatiable thirst for

knowledge. Much of the young Texan's earlier trucu-
lence stemmed from his lack of opportunity to learn
things. Clay Allison's crew might be tough, efficient,
handy with their guns, but they had little to teach Waco.
Since throwing his lot in with the O.D. Connected,
Waco had always been asking questions and found his
new friends willing to take time out to answer, or give
practical demonstrations of things which interested him;
and his chip-on-the-shoulder attitude fell away as he
learned.

Dusty, Waco and Derringer left the office and strolled
along the sidewalk in the direction of Dongelon's
saloon. While none of them expected to find anything
wrong with the games, Derringer figured he could
point out a few things of interest and show the others a
few pointers in the difference between straight and
crooked gambling equipment.

Across the street the Kid came from Birnbaum's store
accompanied by the storekeeper. The problem of Birnbaum's firearms training had been simplified by the
discovery that not only was his wife a real good cook,
but that he possessed a pretty daughter. Once that fact
had been established competition to act as instructor
became keen between Mark and the Kid.

A trio of men rode along the street, passing Dusty's
party and swinging their mounts to halt before the
Wooden Spoon's hitching rail. They were unshaven,
wore cowhand clothes, looked like a bunch of hands
fresh off a trail drive and each wore a low hanging gun.
Leaving their horses with the reins tossed, but not tied,
over the hitching rail, the three men stepped towards the
sidewalk ready to enter the saloon.

After giving the men a quick glance, Waco studied their
horses. The center animal moved restlessly and as it did
Waco saw that its off hind shoe had come loose. He decided to warn the horse's rider, allowing the man a chance
to have the shoe replaced firmly or the horse re-shod.

"Hey, mister!" he called, stepping from the sidewalk alongside Dusty and Derringer. "Hold it a min—"

Turning, the three newcomers looked in Waco's direction, saw the trio of law badges approaching and grabbed at their guns.

"Look out, boy!" Dusty yelled, shooting out his right hand to thrust Waco to one side and sending his left flicking across his body to the off-side Colt.

Two things saved Waco's life that day: Dusty's knowledge of the basic rule of a lawman; and the small Texan's ambidextrous wizardry with his guns.

The center man was very fast. Flame ripped from the barrel of his gun and the bullet missed the staggering Waco by a mere couple of inches. Before the man could fire again or correct his aim, Dusty threw a bullet into him and Dusty shot to kill. There was no other way. The man had shown himself to be better than fair with a Colt and that he had right good reason to fear the approach of lawmen; it paid off only in tombstones to take fool chances with such a man.

Althought the center man was good, the other two were not better than average and they were completely outclassed even by Derringer. Steel rasped on leather as guns came out. Even though off balance, Waco beat Derringer and the other two to shoot. His bullet caught the man at the left in the shoulder and spun him around – but the man still held his gun.

Then Waco learned his second lesson in a few seconds. Dusty threw a shot into the wounded man, spinning him around again. Cocking the seven-and-a-half inch barrelled Army Colt on its recoil, Dusty prepared to shoot again unless the man released his weapon. The impact of Dusty's shot threw the man backwards and his gun clattered to the ground.

Derringer's right hand fanned down and brought out his Colt an instant after Waco fired. Having time to spare – even though it only amounted to a split second –

Derringer sent his bullet into the last of the trio's shoulder and the man staggered back, his heels struck the edge of the sidewalk then he sat down, allowing his gun to fall back from a limp and useless hand.

"Don't shoot!" the man yelled, raising his left hand shoulder high. "Don't shoot, I'm done!"

"Move in on them and watch them!" Dusty ordered and as they walked forward went on. "Boy, never as long as you're wearing a lawman's badge call out to a man, or go towards him after you've stopped him, without being ready to draw your guns."

"I only—"

"I know what you aimed to do and don't blame you for doing it. But innocent as Lon looks, or guilty-looking as hell, don't make the mistake of not being ready to draw. And if you have to draw on a man, keep shooting as long as he holds his gun no matter whether he's standing or lying."

Cold-blooded it might seem, but in later years Waco remembered Dusty's warning and advice and it saved his life on at least one occasion. The youngster had killed four men before that day, each one in a fair fight, but this was the first time he had been in a shooting scrape on the side of the law.

A crowd gathered, people coming from the Wooden Spoon and running along the street. Ignoring them, Dusty told his deputies to gather up the trio's guns. Then he looked down at the three men. The one he shot first was dead; Waco and Dusty's man had wounds and both looked serious; Derringer had been able to merely disarm the third man who looked like it would be some time before he used a gun with his right hand.

"How'd you know?" groaned the third man, holding his shoulder. "Stayley there," he indicated the man Dusty killed, "reckoned word couldn't've got here."

"It arrived," Dusty replied.

"Th – the money's in Stayley's saddle pouches. All of

it just like when we took it out of the Wells Fargo box."

"Where was that?"

"Six miles south of Newt—" the man began, then stopped as he realized how much he had given away.

"A Wells Fargo stage, huh?" Dusty asked.

"I got nothing to say," the man answered.

The Ysabel Kid had arrived on the run, although he found his presence unnecessary. However, Dusty did not let the Kid make a wasted trip for he left the Indian-dark young man to see the removal of the body and arrange for the wounded to be attended by the local doctor then lodged in the cells. Dusty knew he would get nothing more out of the third man, at least not until later, so he let the matter drop. A telegraph message to Newton's Wells Fargo office would give Dusty all the information he needed and the man dropping the name "Stayley" handed Dusty a lead to one of the trio's identity.

What happened was clear enough. The three men held up a Wells Fargo stagecoach out of Newton and came to Mulrooney, possibly by a roundabout route and in a manner which would make tracking them all but impossible. If they had kept their heads when Waco called, they might have got clear through the town of Mulrooney for no word of the holdup had arrived.

Seeing Dongelon among the people who gathered, Dusty went to him and said, "We're just coming in to make a check on the games, Don."

"Feel free anytime," the saloonkeeper replied, leading the way into the Wooden Spoon. "Can I offer you a drink before you start?"

"Not while we're on watch," Dusty answered and turned to Derringer. "Where do you want to start, Frank?"

"How about the roulette table?"

"You're bossing the drive."

Watched by an interested Waco, Derringer examined

the table thoroughly. Although he knew nothing would
be wrong, Derringer removed the table's wheel and
examined the spindle on which it turned. While making
his check, Derringer explained to Waco how un-
scrupulous operators rigged their wheels by means of
hidden springs and wires which worked on a push of a
concealed button so as to ensure that the number most
favorable to the house came up a winner.

"How'd the house make sure the wheel pays off then,
I mean a straight wheel like this one?" Waco asked. "I
don't reckon they can."

"They don't have to even with a straight wheel, b—
Waco."

"How's that?"

"See that sign on the table, house limit twenty-five
cents to twenty-five dollars only. That's how they make
their profit. This's a honest wheel but it gives the house
an edge of five and five-nineteenths per cent. That
means that for every dollar bet, the house collects five
and five-nineteenths cents. Clear?"

"Clear as the Missouri in high-flood."

A grin split Derringer's face for, like Waco, he knew
the Missouri had a reputation for being an exceptionally
muddy river even when not in flood. So to help clear the
subject Derringer explained how the house's percentage
worked, drawing in part of every bet made. He went on
to explain to Waco how the limit protected the house by
preventing the players doubling up on bet after bet until
eventually they won; and also against the chance of a
player walking in, betting a large sum on one roll, win-
ning and walking out with the profits.

"See, bo – Waco," Derringer finished, "you can only
make seven double-up bets then if you lose that last
you'd go over the limit. So you have to make several
small bets and the house gets its rake-off with the percentage. That's fair enough, the owner's supplying a
service and the upkeep of the game costs him money."

"Huh, huh," Waco replied. "I see it now. Let's have a look at the other games, shall we?"

While Waco might see the point of Derringer's argument, he failed entirely to notice the time. So absorbed did he become that the fingers of the clock went moving around as Derringer examined game after game. At each he explained to Waco how it could be fixed so as to ensure the house won heavily and also told the youngster the game's percentage. While giving the decks of cards a casual glance, Derringer warned Waco of the way players at the games tried to improve their luck. All in all Waco was receiving an education in the art of crooked gambling and, as in all the subjects his friends taught him, he stored the information away for future reference.

Just as the three lawmen were leaving the saloon, Mark Counter strolled up to them.

"I thought you was headed for bed?" Dusty asked.

"Was. Only there's a feller down the hall from me who's got a helluva appetite and it worries me."

"Does, huh?"

"Sure. I can figure a man wanting a stack of sandwiches near on two foot high, and a couple of bottles of whisky," Mark drawled. "Only I can't see why he needs half-a-dozen glasses, cigars and pipe tobacco."

"Half-a-dozen, huh?" Dusty grunted. "Let's go."

"This's gone right by me," Waco stated as he followed the other three along the street in the direction of the hotel.

"You'll see, boy," Mark replied.

The manager of the hotel was not present and his desk clerk, a young man fresh from the east, had ideas about the sanctity of the establishment's guests. After hearing Dusty's request, he shook his head and stated that he could only hand over his pass key on the manager's orders.

"It's your door," Dusty drawled.

"How do you mean, Marshal?"

"There's something going on in one of your rooms. When I knock on the door, I may have to go in fast. That means either unlocking and opening the door – or we kick it in. It's your choice, but I sure as hell can't see Mr. Schafer thinking happy about you when he hears why we did it."

One thing the young man learned early in his career as a hotel desk clerk was that any trouble which happened in the building usually wound up as being his fault. In the small town back east he had never seen much of the law, but he guessed that Dusty did not aim to waste time arguing. Either he handed over the pass key or the small Texan's party would break open the door and Schafer, the manager, was sure to hold the desk clerk responsible.

Taking the key, Dusty led the others up the stairs and along the passage to the room Mark pointed out. They halted two on each side of the door, standing back against the wall. Reaching around, Dusty knocked loudly.

"Law here," he shouted. "Open up!"

There was no reply for a moment, so Dusty slipped the pass key into the lock and turned it. Thrusting open the door, Dusty went in fast, followed by the other three. All halted and looked at the scene before them. They saw it through a haze of tobacco smoke; half-a-dozen men seated around a bed and grabbing up money and cards hurriedly.

"There's no law against gambling, gents," Dusty remarked. "Open the window and let's have us some air in here, boy."

While crossing the room, Waco studied the gamblers. Four of them were Texas cowhands and looked like they had only recently paid off a drive. One of the other pair looked like he might be a store-clerk or some other kind of town dweller, an innocent, honest appearing man in a cheap suit. The last of the six showed what he was, a professional gambler and most likely the organizer of the game.

"Then what'd you bust in here for?" asked the gambler sullenly.

"Civic ordinance number thirty-seven, mister," Dusty replied. "It empowers the town marshal to examine any instrument, device or article used for the purpose of gambling."

"This could be a stick-up!" yelped the townsman.

"Don't be *loco*," one of the cowhands replied. "That there's Cap'n Fog and Mark Counter. I rode for them on that drive they made for Rocking H, when they made Wyatt Earp and Bat Masterson run out of Dodge City."*

"Howdy, Vic," Dusty greeted, recognizing the man. "What happened?"

"Gent here," said the cowhand, indicating the gambler, "got him a game up. Said we could play in his room and not have to pay any house charge. This other fellèr here," Vic waved to the townsman, "came along for a game."

"Huh huh!" Dusty grunted. "Check over the cards, Frank."

Dusty knew there would be no trouble from the cowhands now he had been recognized as a friend. Otherwise the townsman's words might have started shooting. Unless Dusty missed his guess – and he didn't reckon he missed – that had been the man's intention when shouting the suggestion of a hold-up.

"Hell, these cards have designs all over their backs," the gambler growled. "Everybody knows you can't mark them."

"That's what your sort want everybody to think,"

* Told in *Trail Boss* by J. T. Edson.

Derringer replied over the other players' rumble of agreement.

Gathering in the cards, Derringer gripped them firmly in his left hand. He ran his right thumb over the upper edge like a child playing with a "moving picture" book, watching the flipped pasteboards intently. When he had repeated the process twice more, Derringer offered the deck to Waco.

"Try that and see what you see, b—"

"For gawd's sake say 'boy' just once," Waco suggested. "You're dang nigh old enough to be my grandpappy anyways."

Derringer grinned as he realized that he had been admitted into the select few who could address Waco with the name "boy" and not wind up fighting.

"Can't see a danged th—" Waco went on, following Derringer's actions with the deck of cards. "Hey though, the pattern's changed—"

"Just sit right there, *hombre!*"

The words cracked out from Dusty's lips and were accompanied by the click of his right hand Colt coming to full cock as he threw down on the gambler and halted the man's move towards his jacket's sleeve. An instant later the townsman found himself with a first-class view of the bore of Mark's right side Colt. Both men were covered and sat very still, all ideas of resisting further comments on the cards forgotten by them.

"You mean they was cheating?" growled one of the cowhands.

"Could be," Dusty replied. "Just you boys sit right there and leave us handle it, huh?"

"You'd best do it, Wilf," Vic warned. "Cap'n Fog's got a right convincing way with him happen you don't."

"How about it, Frank?" Dusty asked.

Taking the cards from Waco, Derringer riffled them once more, inserting a finger in between two of them.

He removed the card and held it towards Dusty and said, "They're what's known as 'block-outs.' There's a lot of people believe there has to be a white border around the design before the cards can be marked. I reckon the idea was started by a tinhorn. See that piece of the diamond patterning on the back? It's been darkened a mite more than the rest and is just a mite out of shape."

Even when pointed out, the blocking-out took some spotting. Both the gambler and his partner must have possessed keen vision to make use of the marking.

"But that deck was new opened, with the Federal Revenue stamp on the outside, Cap'n," Vic objected. "I wouldn't've been loco enough to play otherwise."

"I know two fellers in Kansas City who earn maybe thirty-five dollars a *week* steaming off the Revenue seals, marking the cards then sealing the deck again," Derringer answered.

Surprise showed on the cowhands' – and Waco's – faces. A cowhand only earned thirty-five dollars with a month's hard work.

"Share out all the money that's on the table, boys," Dusty ordered, using the term "table" even though the game had been played on a bed. "And in future if you have to gamble, do it in a saloon. You won't win anyways, but at least there you'll not be cheated out of it."

Chuckling at Dusty's adroit summing up of a man's chances when it came to gambling, the cowhands gathered up the money and started to share it among themselves. As a fair amount of both the gambler and the townsman's money was included in the share-out, the cowhands had no complaints and Dusty knew they would have no desire to seek out and take retaliatory measures against the two men.

Neither of the crooks said a word in protest, but sat scowling and watched the delighted cowhands troop out of the room. Then the gambler asked what would happen to them.

"That depends," Dusty replied. "Search the room, Frank. Waco, help Mark search this pair."

"Keep close to him while you're doing it, boy," Mark prompted, "and lay your guns aside while you do it if there's more than one of you. Let the other man keep the prisoner covered. Another thing, keep your groin, gut and the rest out of the way while you're doing it."

Both Waco and Mark laid aside their guns and let Dusty cover the two tinhorns. Swiftly Mark demonstrated the "pat search" used by lawmen to locate hidden but fairly bulky objects such as weapons. The blond giant worked from behind his man, the gambler, removing a Remington Double Derringer from the man's right sleeve and an ivory-gripped, spear-pointed push dagger with a four-inch blade and a spring-away sheath from up the left. Following Mark's moves, Waco searched the townsman and ensured that his man had no weapons hidden away.

While this went on, Derringer checked the gambler's belongings and on opening a case found what amounted to a small gambling casino; including a miniature roulette wheel and cloth layout, several decks of cards, all marked or otherwise doctored and a few dice which carried loads or were mis-spotted.

"What now?" growled the gambler.

"We're taking you in," Dusty replied. "Do you want to see a lawyer?"

"Does it have to come to a trial?" asked the townsman.

"Don't add attempted bribery to it," Dusty warned. "Take them in, boy. Where do you live, *hombre*?"

"Down at the other hotel," the townsman, to whom Dusty addressed the question, replied sullenly.

"Take him and collect his gear, Mark, Frank. Waco and I'll handle this one."

At the jail Dusty had the two men thoroughly searched and listed their property having them sign the list before locking the items in the office safe, then he consigned the two men to one of the cells. In the morning they would be taken before the judge, have a hefty fine slapped on them and then be seen on their way out of town.

"What'll we do with this, Dusty?" Mark asked, nodding to the case of crooked gambling gear.

"Leave it here," Derringer suggested. "I'll see how much I can teach the boy with it."

"I'd surely hate to grow up all big and ignorant," Waco agreed, giving Mark a studied and knowing glance. "If I did, all I'd be good for'd be chasing ga – Yeeow! Is that clock right?"

All eyes turned to the wall clock. They had been so engrossed in their work that none of them gave a thought to the passing of time. Staring with horrified eyes, Waco tried to imagine the clock's fingers did not show half past seven.

"It's right as the off-side of a horse," Dusty answered and went on innocently, "Was you going some place?"

"You show her who's boss, boy," Mark whooped as the youngster, without offering any answer to Dusty's question, dashed out of the office.

"She *knows* who's boss," Derringer contributed.

Laughing, the three men watched Waco hurry along the sidewalk in the direction of the Fair Lady Saloon.

"He's a good kid," Derringer remarked as they turned from the window.

"He's a damned good *man* to have siding you in a fight," Dusty corrected.

"Yep!" agreed Mark. "He'll do to ride the river with. Now I'm going to the hotel to try and get some sleep."

"Lon's not back yet," Dusty pointed out, then

looked at Derringer. "Was I to be asked, Frank, I'd say you just volunteered for my partner tonight."

"Me?" Derringer croaked. "I'm supposed to be the gambling expert."

"So you are. Get the cards out while things are quiet and we'll have a few hands of crib – and make sure you don't take one of the decks we confiscated from our two guests."

Waco hurried towards the Fair Lady Saloon. A cold feeling came over him as he thought of the waiting girl and he would have been willing to bet all he owned that Babsy was not amused. Fact being she would likely peel his hide off when he arrived.

An indignant looking Babsy stood on the sidewalk before the saloon. She wore a neat little blue dress with a bustle, a picture hat and held a parasol. From the way her dainty right foot tapped on the sidewalk, Waco could tell she was pot-boiling mad and he hoped she would listen to his explanation.

"Well?" Babsy asked.

"I've been working."

"Huh! A likely story. I saw you coming out of the Wooden Spoon!"

"Sure," Waco agreed. "We went in to che—"

"I suppose you think I'm going to fall for that!" Babsy squeaked.

"It's the living truth. I went in with Dusty and Frank Derringer, him being our gambling deputy. Then just as we finished, Mark come along with a crooked poker game and we raided it. One way and ano—"

Again Waco's words trailed off as some instinct warned him that Babsy would not take kindly to the suggestion that he preferred listening to Derringer on the subject of gambling to taking her to supper. Actually Waco did not prefer the former, only Derringer made it so interesting that the youngster lost all track of time.

"Well?" Babsy repeated.

Which same was when Waco began to get annoyed. "I told you I was working late!" he growled. "Now I'm here, right side up and all my buttons on. So let's us go eat supper."

"Just like that?"

"Just like that!"

"Then no thank you, mate!" snorted Babsy. "I'll go to supper myself."

"All right then!" Waco snapped back. "Go to going!"

"Don't worry. I'm going to!"

At which point both Babsy and Waco paused and waited for the other to make a move that would lead them to reconciliation. The trouble being that both of them possessed an almost equal streak of mule; and neither intended to give in first.

After waiting for almost a minute, Babsy gave an angry snort, turned and stamped off along the street. Waco watched her go, standing where he was and scowling at the brightly dressed little figure. Man, that 'lil blonde gal looked as cute as a June-bug and as desirable as anything he could ever remember seeing. Only he failed to see him taking to the idea of any girl – even one as pretty as Babsy – getting all uppy with him.

However, with all the various celebrating men in town it might not be any too safe for Babsy walking the streets alone. While an ordinary town girl would have been fairly safe even from a drunken cowhand, Babsy had become well-known for her singing and dancing act at the Fair Lady. Cowhands and others often formed very wrong impressions of girls who worked in saloons; and that could lead Babsy right straight smack bang into trouble.

Not that Waco gave a damn either which-ways of course, but – well he was a town lawman and Miss

Freddie had kind of made him responsible for the safety and well-being of her main and star performer.

With his excuse made up to his own satisfaction, Waco walked along the street after the girl, keeping some thirty yards or so behind her and making no attempt to catch up with her. He reckoned that by the time they had reached the hotel, Babsy – all right, then, both of them – would have simmered down enough to patch things up and have their supper and buggy ride.

Babsy knew that Waco followed her and reached much the same conclusion. All might have gone as planned if a brace of handsome, celebrating young Texas cowhands had not come from a store and removed their hats gravely as the girl approached. They had paid off from their herd the previous day and carried a mite more liquor than was good for them; although not so much that they failed to recognize the little girl who amused and charmed them the previous night at the Fair Lady.

"Howdy, ma'am," the taller of the pair greeted. "I'm Tad, 'n' this's Beck."

"We saw your show last night," Beck told her seriously "Sure was good."

"Sure was," agreed Tad.

I'll teach that there Waco! Babsy thought and then said, "Did you like it enough to take me to supper?"

"Now you sure got a good idea there, ma'am," agreed Tad.

From the start Babsy figured she might be going too far. While the two cowhands behaved politely at first, they grew more familiar as the meal – and liquor – progressed. The girl tried to attract Waco's attention as he sat silently eating a meal across the room, but he refused to be drawn into what he knew must wind up in a fight. Not that Waco feared a fight. He felt a sense of responsibility and knew becoming involved in a public brawl was not the action a good lawman took.

At last the meal ended and Babsy hoped to get away from the two cowhands so as to go and make her peace with Waco. However, Tad and Beck each took an arm and led her out on to the street. Night had fallen, with a moon throwing some light on the street. To Babsy's horror there were few people about and the two cowhands began to steer her towards the Fair Lady.

"How's about a kiss?" asked Tad.

"Not on the street!" Babsy gasped, which was a mistake.

"That's easy settled," grinned the cowhand and nodded to the alley between the hotel and its neighbouring building. "Let's go down there."

Before Babsy could raise any objections, the two cowhands had taken her into the alley. Tad swung her around, curling his hands around her. Up drove Babsy's knee and Tad let go faster than he took hold, staggering back.

"Looks like she fancies me, Tad boy," grinned Beck and gripped the girl by her shoulders, making sure he kept his side to her knee.

A feeling of panic hit Babsy as the cowhand's face came down towards her. Once back in England a drunken footman at Freddie's house caught the little girl and tried to kiss her. Only Freddie's arrival and a hard-applied riding crop saved Babsy from the possibility of something worse – but this time Freddie was nowhere around. The fumes of whisky came down into Babsy's face, making her gag and stopping her crying for help.

"G – get off me!" she gasped.

"Shuckens, stop playing hard to get," Beck replied. "I only—"

"You heard the lady!"

Never, not even with the arrival of Freddie that time

in England, had Babsy been so pleased to see a friend come to her aid. She heard Waco's words and saw the tall youngster grab Beck by the shoulder, heaving him bodily backwards.

"Coo – look out!"

Babsy began to thank Waco and yelled a warning an instant too late as Tad lunged forward and crashed his fist into the side of Waco's jaw. Waco went sideways and hit the hotel's wall. Even as he struck the wall, Waco had his right hand gun in his hand. In almost the same move, as Tad sprang forward once more, the gun went back into leather. Waco could not see Dusty wanting any part of a deputy or a friend who shot down a drunken young cowhand without a whole heap better reason than Tad presented at the moment.

On the way north Mark had taught Waco some of the basic fist-fighting techniques, not as much as the youngster would eventually know, but sufficient for the present situation. Waco side-stepped Tad's rush, avoiding the cowhand's blow and ripped his left fist into Tad's unprotected belly. Taken by surprise, Tad folded over but his forward impetus carried him on so his head struck the wall.

Beck moved in as Tad collapsed to the ground. A bellyfull of whisky might give a man the desire to fight, but it sure as hell did not improve his ability or technique. Ducking under Beck's wild blow, Waco came up, ripping home an uppercut that lifted the cowhand on to his toes and draped him flat on his back.

Feet thudded and two shapes came into the mouth of the alley.

"Hold it right there!" Dusty's voice barked.

Attracted by the sound of the fight, while making their rounds, Dusty and Derringer had come to investigate. Shaking his right hand to restore the feeling robbed by its collision with Beck's jaw, Waco turned to speak with his friends.

"It's all right, Dusty," he said.

"What happened?" Dusty asked.

"Boys got a mite festive – with good cause," the youngster growled; and even in the dark Babsy could tell he did not eye her with pleasure or favor.

"Do you want for us to take them in?"

"No, Dusty. Just make sure they're not hurt too bad and tell them I'm sorry," Waco replied, then caught Babsy by the wrist. "Come on, you."

Not until they had passed around the rear of the hotel and stood behind the next building did Babsy try to stop herself being dragged along.

"Here, lay off!" she squawked. "You're hurting—"

Swinging the girl to face him, Waco scowled down at her. They stood behind a store and a number of packing cases of various sizes had been stacked against the wall.

"You little fool!" he growled. "Those two kids are fresh off the trail. For over a month they've not seen a gal. Then you have to come along, making eyes at them and getting the wrong ideas going in their heads. I damned near killed one of them back there. And for what, because you wanted to rile me."

"You ne – Oh, Waco! I wish I'd never listened when the other girls told me to keep you waiting and come down late."

"*You* came out late?"

"I – I'd only just come when you arrived."

A sudden fury rose inside Waco, reaction to his having so nearly come to killing a man – and with so little cause. He might have forgiven Babsy for taking on at being kept waiting; but to find that she had not been kept waiting at all – While he had a damned good reason for coming late, the same could not be said of her and she took on like she was standing out front of the Fair Lady for the full half hour.

"Here, what're you looking at me like that for?" Babsy asked as he gripped her wrist and sat down on one of the packing cases. "What's the gam – Oh no! Waco, you wouldn't – Eeeyow!"

With a jerk, Waco brought the little girl belly down across his knee. He could see that the bustle would impede his actions, so hauled up her frock's skirt and shoved the figure-improver out of the way, exposing the short-legged black drawers, two strips of white thigh streaked with black suspender straps, and black stockinged legs. It made a pretty sight if Waco had felt like admiring the view. Instead of admiring, he ignored it. The hard palm of his hand rose and fell in a rhythmic tattoo on the appropriate part of Babsy's anatomy and to the accompaniment of her squeals of pain. Finally he set her down on her feet and rose.

"Goodnight," he said.

Sniffing down her tears, rubbing her rump and adjusting her clothes, Babsy stared after the departing youngster. Then she took a step forward, stumbled and gave a little wail.

"Oooh! My ankle. Waco, I hurt my ankle!"

Coming back, Waco caught the girl and supported her. "How bad is it?"

"Oooer! I don't think I can walk on it. Can you help me back home?"

Scooping the girl into his arms, he carried her behind the houses to the rear of the Fair Lady Saloon. Babsy took her key to the rear door from her vanity bag, forgetting that she had lost her parasol when the cowhands took her into the alley. Still cradled in Waco's arms, she opened the door and then curled her arms around his neck again, snuggling her face against his shoulder. After locking the door on the inside, she let Waco carry her up to and into her room. Reaching over his shoulder, she closed and bolted the door after them.

Ten minutes later a female Cockney voice might have been heard to say, "Coo-er! You haven't half got a lot of hair on your chest."

And a male Texas voice answered, "You haven't any on yours."

Another part of Waco's education was being completed.

CHAPTER NINE

A Rival for Miss Woods

"Hey, Dusty!" Waco greeted as he walked into the main office at eleven o'clock on Saturday morning. "The new folks at that saloon down Main Street have arrived, from the look of it."

"Have, huh?" Dusty answered, looking up from where he sat writing out the desk log. "You're late getting in."

"Was a mite late getting up this morning," the youngster replied. "Where're the others?"

"Mark and Lon're making the first rounds of the day, Frank's seeing off the two tinhorns we brought in yesterday."

"What happened to them in court?"

"Fined two hundred and fifty dollars each, which same left them with about enough to pay their stage coach fare to Newton. I'll say one thing for the judge, he sure doesn't waste any time. They go in and are fined almost in the same breath, and he makes the fines just the right amount, too."

This did not surprise Waco for he knew that Dusty and the judge met on the first day before court, arranging a schedule of fines for the various minor offenders brought up each morning.

"Have fun on the buggy ride?" Dusty inquired.

"Softest buggy I ever did ride," Waco told him.

"How's about those two cowhands I had the run in with over Babsy last night?"

"We brought 'em 'round and they apologized to you and Babsy in your absence, then went to collect their horses and head out to their outfit's camp. Didn't I hear somebody getting spanked last night?"

"When?" asked Waco innocently.

"Right after you hauled Babsy out of sight; and before you say 'Where?' it was behind the store next to the hotel."

"Now who'd go spanking a lady? Say, let's go look over these new folks. Tolerable fine outfit they've come in with, four wagons of it."

Laying aside the desk's pen, Dusty crossed the room and took his hat from the peg in passing. With Waco at his side, he strolled along the street towards the building where four wagons stood in line. There were several empty buildings of various types along Main Street, but each day the number grew smaller as people flocked in to the prosperous and busy trail end town. It appeared that there would be another saloon competing for trade; and from the way men and women hurried back and forward, carrying tables, chairs and other equipment, the new owner intended to commence the competition as soon as possible.

Dusty recognized the big, buxom blonde woman who stood on the sidewalk and directed operations. Clearly the recognition was mutual for she smiled and came forward, holding out her right hand.

"Howdy, Cap'n Fog," she greeted. "I heard tell you'd been made marshal down here. Gilgore's the name, they call me Buffalo Kate."

"Right pleased to meet you, ma'am," Dusty replied, taking the woman's hand. "Thanks for your warning that day back to Brownton."

"Think nothing of it. You'd the whip-hand of that bunch but I didn't know if you'd recognized Fagan and took him for an honest lawman. I guess what you'd do when you left town, even before I saw Waldo Burkman and the other cattle-buyers pulling out. Anyways, Grief, the mayor up to Brownton, had been after me to cut him in as a non-paying profit-drawing partner. So I took up an offer Frenchie Lefarge made me for my place. Sold out to him afore he realized Mulrooney was getting all the trade. Set my aim down here, bought this place and here I am."

At that moment Freddie came from the Fair Lady and walked along the street then crossed over and came towards Buffalo Kate's wagon. Freddie wore her town clothes and felt dog-tired for the previous nights had been hectic with late hours. The noise of Kate's party arriving had disturbed Freddie's sleep and on rising, the lady mayor of Mulrooney decided she might as well go over to meet the new arrivals. If the newcomers needed help in settling down, Freddie hoped to be able to supply it. She also hoped that she might be able to bring up the subject of how she expected Mulrooney tradespeople to act.

"Hello," she greeted. "Good morning, Dusty."

"Morning, Freddie," Dusty replied. "This's Miss Gilgore, Miss Gilgore, meet Miss Woods."

"Hi there, girlie," Kate said. "Come over to size us up and find out how much trade we'll take away from you?"

"Not exactly," Freddie answered a trifle coldly for she had not liked the other woman's tone.

Buffalo Kate had some considerable experience in running a saloon in a western town. Every instinct she possessed warned her that the young woman before her could be a dangerous rival in a business sense. She also figured out that Freddie was not merely an ordinary saloon girl. Nor had the friendly way Freddie greeted Dusty passed unnoticed. Most likely that prissy-talking limey dude came over to impress her rival saloon-keeper with the fact that she was on first-name terms with the town marshal. So Kate aimed to show that she did not let other folk's friends worry her.

"Say," she said, waving a hand towards the Fair Lady. "Do you work at that trap over there?"

"I happen to own the Fair Lady," Freddie answered.

"Land-sakes," Kate gasped in well-simulated surprise. "What next?"

"And what might that mean?" asked Freddie.

"I've heard of dudes buying up ranches, but never of one *trying* to run a saloon."

"There are some people who say I do pretty well at it," Freddie stated.

"Sure," Kate replied, "but up to now you've had no competition."

"Have I any now?" Freddie asked. "I heard that somebody had bought this place to run as a saloon, but I – oh, you mean this ju – stuff you're taking in is to be used as fixtures for a saloon?"

Watching the two women, Dusty could almost see the sparks flying. He gave a glance at Waco and saw the youngster grinning. Maybe it struck Waco as being amusing but Dusty figured he could get along very well without two feuding saloon-keepers – and them a pair of real nice, friendly women unless roused.

If Freddie had been less tired she might have avoided any stirring of trouble with Buffalo Kate. Maybe – only maybe. Freddie came from a fighting stock; of a breed which won their fortune in the first place with their courage and swords and enlarged it while helping build Britain into the great country it was at that time. So Freddie would not back down from any challenge; and she knew that the gauntlet had been thrown down between them.

"By the way, Miss Gilgore," Freddie went on after a brittle silence of almost a minute. "I happen to be mayor of Mulrooney and we have certain ordinances designed to keep out the riff-raff and unruly elements.

One of the ordinances allows the marshall to inspect all gambling equipment any time he wishes to.''

"Has he inspected your games yet?'' Kate countered.

A flush crept over Freddie's cheeks as she realized that Dusty had not yet inspected her gambling games. So much happened on the previous afternoon after the appointment of Frank Derringer as gambling consultant that Dusty did not find time to check the Fair Lady's games. Nor, if it came to a point, did he see the need to do so in any great hurry as he knew Freddie ran everything fair and above board.

"*My* games are open to inspection as we're erecting them, Cap'n Fog,'' Kate said, after allowing a pause for Freddie to make some excuse. "Of course I realize that wouldn't apply to everybody.''

"You'll come on over and inspect my games right now, Du – Captain Fog!'' Freddie snorted. "And ask this person to send one of her house gamblers along to help you. When dealing with the lower elements one has to prove everything to their limited satisfaction.''

Now it appeared to be Kate's turn to redden up in anger. A cold glint came to Kate's eyes and she studied Freddie. Not even the loose sleeved white blouse and doeskin divided skirt could hide the strength and firm-fleshed power of Freddie's body from Kate and the blonde found, not entirely to her surprise, that she did not face a milk-soft dude but a woman as tough and capable as herself. Kate realized that they had taken the matter as far as they could without reaching a point where neither could back out of a physical brawl. Knowing something of western towns, Kate had more sense than to start brawling with a business rival in the open street on the day of her arrival. There only remained one thing – yet probably the most difficult thing of all, to get out of the situation without loss of face or appearing to back down.

"Ladies,'' Dusty said, realizing how far the affair had gone and offering the women a way out. "I'll send

Waco to relieve Frank Derringer and then we'll go over to the Fair Lady while Miss Gilgore—''

"Make it Kate, Cap'n, I'll be around here for a fair time," the blonde interrupted, throwing a defiant glance at Freddie.

"While Kate gets her place set up," Dusty put in hurriedly. "Loan me one of your house dealers, Kate, to go over the Fair Lady with Derringer."

"Shuckens, Cap'n, I trust *you*."

"I insist you send one!" Freddie snapped.

"Yeah!" bristled Kate. "And who—"

"Likely Miss Kate can't spare anybody, her crowd all working so hard," Waco remarked, doing the right thing instinctively.

His words offered both Freddie and Kate a face-saver and neither looked entirely unhappy about it.

"Say, Freddie," Dusty put in, mentally blessing Waco for the words. "I asked the trail bosses to be at the jail at noon. Can you go put up the idea we discussed last night to them while I do my work?"

Slowly Freddie unclenched her tight-closed right hand. She gave a sniff and nodded her agreement. At last she had been given a chance to withdraw without it appearing that the fat, over-stuffed blonde ran her off. Her sense of responsibility alone would have made her attend to a civic duty anyway; which was what Dusty counted on when he made the suggestion.

"What's all that about?" Kate asked, watching Freddie walk away.

"The saloons aren't allowed to open on Sunday and the sale of liquor is banned for the day. So we figured to give the cowhands a chance to show off a mite to the town folks and take their minds off not being able to drink and whoop things up in town."

"Your idea?"

"Part mine, part Freddie's," Dusty admitted.

"Who is she?"

"Her name's Freddie Woods, she helped found the

town and folks elected her mayor. She's a real nice gal."

"Yeah?" sniffed Kate. "Well, she gets no-place faster than that with me."

"Why?" Dusty asked.

"Huh?" replied Kate, looking confused. "I – she – excuse me, Cap'n. I've gotta hurry my folks on happen I hope to open tonight."

Watching Kate walk away, Dusty grinned faintly and Waco asked what might be amusing his *amigo*.

"Those two, pawing dirt and sharpening their horns," Dusty explained and glanced at the left side of the youngster's neck. "Your bandana's slipping, boy."

Waco gave a guilty start and reached up to raise the bandana so that it covered the oval-shaped bruise on the side of his neck.

"If you-all so smart," he said to hide his confusion, "tell lil ignorant me why they don't get along. They look a whole lot alike to me, in their ways, I mean."

"Lil ignorant you's asked the question and answered it," Dusty grinned. "You never saw the two biggest bulls in a herd get along together, did you?"

"Not until they'd locked horns and got to know who was best," Waco admitted. "Hey! You don't reckon Miss Freddie and Buffalo Kate'll lock horns, do you?"

"I hope not, boy," Dusty replied with feeling. "I surely hope not. Go find Frank Derringer and send him up here."

Neither of the saloon checks proved more than Dusty already knew in one case and guessed in the other, that both Freddie and Kate ran straight games and relied solely on the house's percentage to give them their profit.

A party of townsmen arrived to lend Kate's workers a hand in setting up the saloon ready for opening in the evening. Although Kate did not learn the fact until much later, it had been Freddie who suggested that the men lent a hand at making their new fellow-citizen welcome.

One word from Freddie would have blasted Buffalo Kate's chances of success, but the word did not come out. Freddie knew she had a serious rival in business and aimed to try to lick the more experienced woman on their mutual ground without taking advantage of her civic position or social popularity.

Although Freddie had brought in one of the best known and most popular acts which played the Southern States, she would have been willing to close for the Saturday night and let Buffalo Kate's opening go unchallenged. However, on Freddie's return from the meeting with the trail bosses – after making satisfactory arrangements for the Sunday entertainment – she met Buffalo Kate. Words were exchanged and as a result Freddie determined to open and teach Kate a lesson.

"Let the battle commence!" she said as she entered the Fair Lady.

Althought Kate drew in some trade, the bulk went to Freddie despite the novelty of the blonde's opening night. The drawing power of Freddie's star act pulled in Texans like iron filings to a magnet. At just over midnight, with the saloon closed, Buffalo Kate checked her takings and looked at her head bartender.

"That gal's going to make things tough," she said in an admiring tone. "Yes sir, Wally, we've a fight on our hands here. If she wants war, by cracky, she's going to get it."

The bartender nodded his agreement. One thing he figured out, that limey gal might be good, but he sure couldn't see her licking his boss.

To offset boredom and the accompanying chance for the devil to find work that idle hands might do, Dusty and Freddie, with the agreement and support of the local preacher, had arranged a series of contests for the various cowhands and outfits in and around town. Several unbroken horses were obtained to try out riding skill; a course complete with a number of jumps laid out for horse races; a range rigged to allow the running of shooting matches. For a day the cowhands would be entertaining the local citizens and everybody looked forward to this pleasant change. The cowhands felt pleased with a chance to show off their skills and the townsfolk anticipated seeing some of the things they read of cowhands doing in the course of their range work.

With the exception of Mark, who volunteered to run the office, Dusty had all his deputies on hand to keep an eye on the way things went. They were told to mingle with the crowd, watch out for illicit liquor selling and any attempts at gambling. In one way the idea was excellent; yet it also gave an indirect cause to the saloon feud being resumed when for a time it seemed that the affair might fade and be forgotten.

Having heard much of Freddie's work in establishing and handling the town, Buffalo Kate was a good enough sport to admit the English girl had something and so greeted her affably enough when they met. For her part Freddie was willing to be friends and introduced Kate to the leading civic dignitaries.

The dove of peace let out a sigh of content and glided down to land, then—

"Hello there, handsome!"

Turning, Waco looked at the speaker by his side. She was a small, shapely and very pretty red-headed girl. From her clothes Waco figured her to be a saloon worker but had an uneasy feeling that he could not remember seeing her at either the Fair Lady or the Wooden Spoon. Which same meant she must come from the Buffalo.

"Say, you're cute," the girl went on. "You must be the handsome young one the girls told me about. My name's Ginger."

"And mine's Babsy," hissed a voice from Waco's other side.

"So what?" Ginger asked, eyeing Babsy up and down in contempt.

"So Waco's my boyfriend, that's what!"

Although he had never sat on a keg of gunpower with a burning fuse running to it, Waco discovered how one would feel while doing so. The two pretty little girls, alike in height and shape, glared at each other like a pair of cats on a back-alley fence.

"You foreigners haven't any right to come over here grabbing our men!" Ginger spat out.

"Foreigner!" squealed Babsy, for to her insular British mind no matter where in the world she might be it was always the other folk who were the foreigners. "I'll do some hairgrabbing, not man-grabbing!"

"So grab away!" Ginger challenged, clenching her fists.

For once in his life Waco did not know what to do for the best. Neither girl gave him a second glance and a crowd gathered in a circle around them, grinning in eager anticipation. A hair-yanking brawl between a couple of pretty and real lively-looking little girls would add spice and make memorable the day's entertainment; and those two looked like they would put up a humdinger of a battle.

Only it did not come to a fight.

A hand caught Babsy's hand even as the little girl prepared to light down on Ginger with flying fists.

"That's enough, Babsy!" Freddie snapped in a carrying voice. "I realize you were provoked, but one has to expect that sort of thing from their kind."

"Easy, Ginger!" ordered Kate, glowering at Freddie and also raising her voice. "You don't want to let that sort bother you."

The white dove of peace flapped wearily back into the sky; it figured it would not be needed around Mulrooney for a spell.

Girls from both saloons mingled in the watching crowd and the situation had explosive overtones. One wrong move would see an unholy, scrapping tangle that could involve everybody around. Dusty saw that as he came through the crowd, shoving a path through despite of the fact that many taller men stood in his way.

"Come on, Waco," Babsy said.

"Let's go see the horse races, handsome," Ginger put in.

Dusty took the matter out of Waco's hands.

"Go relieve Mark at the jail, boy," he ordered. "Miss Freddie, would you and Babsy go start the horse races? And I'd like you and Ginger to help the judges on the finishing line and hand out the prizes to the winners, Miss Kate."

Once again the two women were handed a face-saver that prevented them taking the matter beyond the point of no return. Freddie and Kate led off their fuming employees and the crowd broke up.

"Dang females!" Waco snorted. "I'll never understand women."

"Boy," Dusty replied. "They do say that's a common complaint among men."

For the rest of the afternoon, while the cowhand sporting events went on, Dusty and his deputies kept on the move. Freddie and Kate's girls glared at each other whenever they met and only by keeping constantly on the alert did Dusty's deputies maintain peace. One thing worried Dusty at first; his female deputy might be expected to show partisanship to her friends of the Fair Lady. In this he did not need to worry for Freddie's orders to Big Sarah had been definite and the big woman would not think of disobeying. So Sarah let her fellow-workers know that in the matter of inter-saloon rivalry she aimed to stay neutral and do her duty as an officer of the law. When the girls took a complaint to Freddie, she told them straight that Sarah's actions met with her complete approval and there the matter ended.

A tired and not entirely unhappy group of peace officers gathered in the jail that evening.

"Man!" said the Kid in a heart-felt manner. "I sure never want another day like that again."

"Or me," Big Sarah groaned, removing her shoes. "I

thought we'd have some real bad trouble once or twice.''

"It was rough on you having to go against your pards like that," Dusty remarked. "Thanks, Sarah."

"Don't thank me," she grinned. "It's not over yet, Cap'n. There's going to be a tangle between Miss Freddie and that Buffalo Kate and when it comes, it'll make the battle at Bearcat Annie's in Quiet Town look like a Sunday-school picnic."

Recalling the famous battle in Bearcat Annie's saloon; when three women deputies slugged it out with the saloon-keeper and her girls, allowing the male members of the law to slip into the saloon unnoticed; Dusty nodded his agreement. He, too, could see trouble ahead and figured that when it finally blew – man, it would blow like a Texas twister.

CHAPTER TEN

A Visitor from Brownton

Dusty entered the office after what had become a regular morning visit to Freddie Woods's rooms at the Fair Lady. It was Monday morning and as yet the two rival saloons had not opened for business. Just as Dusty came in through the rear door, Wally, Buffalo Kate's head bartender, burst in at the front.

"We got trouble, Cap'n Fog!" he said. "Frenchie Lefarge just come into town with half-a-dozen gun-hands at his back. He's got a hate on Kate for selling out to him at Brownton."

Without wasting any time Dusty gave his orders, or order for he said only one word.

"Shotguns!"

Springing to the rack, Waco handed a double-barreled, ten-gauge shotgun to Frank Derringer, passed a second to Dusty and carried one for himself and another for the Kid. By that time the Kid had broken out a box of shells from the desk drawer and each man took a handful. Loading their guns as they went, the four lawmen headed towards where a buckboard and several horses stood before the Buffalo Saloon.

In the saloon Buffalo Kate looked at the tall, slim, swarthily handsome Frenchie Lefarge, then glanced at the six gun-hung hard-cases who stood behind him. Even had any of her male staff been present, she doubted if they could handle those professional gun-hands.

"You sold me your place in Brownton, Kate," Lefarge said.

"And you'd been asking me to, even making veiled threats," she replied. "I might have got scared."

"Or you might have heard something," Lefarge purred. "To keep us friendly, I will become your partner."

"You?" Kate snorted. "You'd not last five minutes in this town, Lefarge. This's a clean town and they don't stand for crooked gamblers."

"You are being insulting, my Kate. Don't make me angry. And as to this town, I have yet to see a lawman who would not look the other way for a price."

"Just turn around and start looking at one, *hombre*," said a soft-drawled Texas voice from the door.

Lefarge had six men at his back. Half-a-dozen men who reckoned to be handy with their guns, yet not one of them made a move. Even as Dusty Fog stepped through the front door, three more men made their appearance at the left side, right hand and rear entrances to the barroom. Every one of the quartet held a shotgun and the hard-cases recalled the old range saying, "There's always a burying when buckshot's used." None of the men were naïve enough to believe the guns held anything other than a load of nine .32 caliber buckshot balls per barrel; and the hard-cases would be caught in a veritable hail of those deadly balls if any of them made a wrong move.

"And who asked you to interfere?" Lefarge growled, seeing his men did not intend to make any moves.

"I heard you say every lawman has his bribe price, *hombre*," Dusty replied. "I'm telling you that you're a liar."

"That's a hard word!"

"Which's why I used it."

"I see. I see," Lefarge purred. "Now I am supposed to grab at a gun and be shot down, is that the idea?"

"Not entirely, but it'll do until I get a better one," Dusty replied.

"You're quite a brave *little* man behind those guns," Lefarge said in a loud voice which carried to the small crowd of people who gathered outside the saloon. "And so you should be, for you are a master with a gun. But any fool can pull a trigger. It takes a man to handle a duelling sword."

"Don't do it, Cap'n!" Buffalo Kate warned.

"And you are a man?" asked Dusty, ignoring the warning and making for the trap opened by Lefarge.

"I am."

"And I'm not?"

A mocking smile played on Lefarge's lips. The old technique looked to be working as well as always. One could rely on these stupid cowhand gun-fighters to leap at the bait without thinking of the consequences.

"There would be a good way of proving it," he purred.

"Sure would – if we had any of those duelling swords here," Dusty agreed.

With the sudden lash, like the jaws of a steel bear trap clamping on their unsuspecting victim, Lefarge brought off his coup.

"I have a pair in my buckboard. Now, unless you are afraid to back your words, I will send one of my men to collect them."

"Send him ahead, but no tricks," Dusty replied.

"And if I kill you, what action will your friends take?"

"None at all. You hear that, Lon, Waco, Frank?"

"We heard," growled the Kid and the other two gave their agreement.

All of which came as a shock to Lefarge. He never expected Dusty to accept the challenge once hearing that swords were readily available. In that case the small

Texan would be finished in town, laughed out as a fool who boasted and feared to back his words. However, the end result would be the same if Dusty fought. He was going to die and the Brownton crowd had a way open for them to move in and take Mulrooney over as a going concern.

One of the men left the saloon and returned with a long wooden box which he opened to expose a pair of fine-looking duelling swords. Lefarge offered Dusty first choice of weapons and the small Texan reached into the box to take out one of the swords. From the first moment Dusty realized that the sword felt all wrong. It did not balance correctly in his hand, the blade seeming to be too long and the hilt incorrectly shaped. The sword would be hell to anybody who had not used it regularly. That was an old professional duellist's trick; having the swords built in such manner gave their regular handler a big edge over his opponent.

"Is something wrong?" asked Lefarge as Dusty laid down the sword again.

"Sure. I don't like that one."

"Edging out, little man?" Lefarge sneered, removing his fancy vest and laying it on the jacket he had already taken off and placed on a table.

"Nope. Lon, go ask Freddie to loan me one of her swords – if this *hombre* can wait a few minutes."

"As long as I get my fight I can wait," the Frenchman replied.

Ten minutes later Freddie arrived with the Kid and carrying one of the swords from her rooms. She asked no questions, the scene told her all she wished to know, but handed the sword hilt first to Dusty and watched him remove the safety button from its tip.

A puzzled frown crept over Lefarge's face as he watched the casually easy manner Dusty handled the sword. It appeared that the Texan had some knowledge of fencing. Of course, that would not save him. What chance did a cowhand stand against a man who learned fencing under a New Orleans master?

He learned the answer to that question soon enough. One glance told him that the small Texan knew more than a little about fencing and a couple of passes after the fight started warned Lefarge that he was matched against a man almost his equal with a sword.

If it came to a point, Dusty had a slight advantage over Lefarge. Back in the Rio Hondo he could always practise with his cousins, all of whom had received fencing training. More than that; since his arrival in Mulrooney, Dusty had worked out with the swords each morning against Freddie, and the girl could handle a blade very well. Against this Lefarge had little chance of practising, for there were few people he knew who could fence. So if anything Dusty was better trained, and in far better physical shape, than the duellist.

Steel hissed and sang in the Buffalo Saloon. At first Dusty retreated before Lefarge's attack and allowed the man to drive him across the room. Dusty fought a defensive action, waiting until he got the measure of his man. Then, with his back almost touching the wall, Dusty changed his tactics. From defense he went into attack and Lefarge recoiled as if drawn back on a spring. Fear flickered on the man's face as he fought desperately back. A parry began and too late Lefarge saw he had been tricked into trying to stop a feint. Before he could make up his mind what to do, he felt a shocking sensation in his left side and he stiffened on his toes, his sword clattering from his hand.

Dusty withdrew his sword with a quick smooth jerk and the man collapsed at his feet. A momentary silence fell over the crowd who had entered the saloon to see the fight. Then eager chatter rose and every eye went to the small Texan who once more had proved himself to be the equal and better of a much larger man.

"Best get a doctor for him," Dusty said, holding the

bloody sword point down and turning towards the Kid.

"The undertaker'd be more use," the Kid replied. "You got him through the heart, or I'm no knife-fighter."

And the Kid's guess proved to be correct. When the town's doctor arrived he found a corpse waiting for him.

"You bunch come into town with him," Dusty said to the gunmen.

"Sure," one of them replied.

"Then take him back to Brownton for burying."

Watching the gunmen leave town with the still shape in the buckboard, Dusty wiped the blade of Freddie's sword.

"What happened, Dusty?" Freddie asked, coming to the small Texan's side.

"His name was Lefarge, he was a tinhorn who used that sword on anybody who tried to call him down. Came to town to try and force Miss Kate into taking him on as a partner."

"And he was no friend of mine," Kate put in.

"I never thought he was," Freddie replied.

Once more the olive branch was waved. Freddie and Kate became almost friendly. In fact, the friendship lasted until nightfall.

Mayor Grief was a worried man as he stood outside his office with Marshal Banks Fagan at his side. For the past few days Fagan had been growing restless, for the expected profits of his office had not made their appearance. However, Frenchie Lefarge ought to be able to get rid of Dusty Fog once and f—

"Look there!" he croaked and pointed to the approaching party.

Both Grief and Fagan recognized the riders as being the men Lefarge took with him, yet they could see no sign of the gambler in his buckboard – unless that blanket-draped shape – no, it could not be.

But it was. The gunman driving the buggy waved a

hand to the shape and said unnecessarily, "Frenchie's dead. Dusty Fog took him on with swords and killed him."

"But that's impossible!" croaked Grief.

"Yeah," the gunman replied dryly. "That's what Frenchie thought – only he was wrong, too. We'll take him to the undertaker's."

Watching the party go by, Grief let out a blistering string of curses. He raved on about the evils of fate that brought Dusty Fog into his town and drove all the trade away from it. For a time Fagan let Grief carry on, then he gave a grin.

"How much would it be worth to break Mulrooney?" he asked.

"Could it be done?"

"I reckon it could. See, I've had a man hanging around Mulrooney and watching the way things went. He told me something interesting."

"What's that?"

"Let's go into your office and talk, it's more private."

Inside the mayor's office, a well-furnished room with more luxury than most civic authorities in the west could claim, the two men sat on opposite sides of the desk and Grief took out the office bottle and box of cigars.

"You aim to give them trouble down there?" he asked.

"I thought of that – and tossed it out," Fagan admitted. "Those Texans are too handy a bunch to let things get out of hand. Only there's a way we can break Mulrooney."

"How?"

"What'd happen if the bank got taken for every dime in its vault?"

"Could it be done?" Grief breathed.

"I reckon it could. See, my man tells me there's some fuss brewing between Buffalo Kate and that gal who owns the Fair Lady. If things go the way I reckon they might, knowing Kate, there's a chance my plan'll work.''

"Do you reckon that the bank could be hit in daylight?''

"I've got something figured out," Fagan replied. "Only it may take a week or so to set it up."

"How're you going to do it?'' Grief inquired, a shade too innocently for Fagan's taste.

"My way,'' replied the marshal.

Grief could get no more out of Fagan. Although the marshal had all the details of his plan worked out, he doubted if he would be wise to let Grief know too much. It did not pay to take unnecessary chances when dealing with a tricky cuss like the mayor of Brownton; especially when a man aimed to make a fair amount of money out of him.

CHAPTER ELEVEN

The Challenge

"Is the Pride of Dixie appearing at your place tonight Freddie?" Kate asked during their period of friendship following the departure of Lefarge's men.

"No. I could only get him for one night. He's booked into a place in Brownton tonight."

"I thought I saw him in town yesterday?"

"So you did," Freddie replied. "He's still at the hotel and plans to go up to Brownton on the noon train."

Never had Kate fought to keep any trace of emotion showing in her voice or on her face as she did at that moment. Keeping her tones calm, she remarked, "I'd best go check on my bar stock to see what replacements I need."

"I've some work to do, too. How do you like the town?"

"It's great, one of the best I've ever been in."

"'I won't say it!" Freddie thought. "I'll stay friendly."

"I almost hate myself for doing this," Kate thought as Freddie walked away. "But it'll teach her a lesson and show her who's the best saloon owner."

Freddie's friendly feeling lasted until the evening when she heard that the Pride of Dixie was appearing at the Buffalo for two nights. As clearly as if it lay written before her, Freddie saw what must have happened. On learning the Pride was still in town, Kate visited him and must have told him what sort of place he had booked into next. Then Kate offered to hire him to appear in her place and had the best drawing attraction possible. Trade was not very brisk in the Fair Lady that night and the noise from the Buffalo made it far worse.

"Babsy, Vera, Jill, Rita!" Freddie called and the girls gathered around her. "Are you game to put one over on the Buffalo crowd tomorrow?"

"Aren't we though?" Babsy replied.

Word passed around the town during Monday evening and throughout Tuesday that some of Freddie's girls had quarrelled over a poker game and would play out a match the Tuesday evening to decide who was best. Freddie saw to it that word of the stakes the girls played for would reach the right ears. Not even the Pride of Dixie could compete with the sight of four pretty girls playing poker for their clothes upon the Fair Lady's stage.

Dusty saw no cause to interfere for he reckoned that Freddie had good sense enough to know when to have her girls stop the betting. In this he proved correct. The girls bet and removed right down to their scanty underwear but on the final bet the stage's curtain dropped. Before her audience could become restless, Freddie had drinks on the house called and started her show.

Wednesday found both saloons starting without a top-name drawing card and Kate's girls appeared in even shorter than usual dresses. By opening time on Thursday night Freddie's girls entertained their customers wearing skirts that barely reached below their stocking tops. News of this reached the Buffalo and saw Kate's girls heading for their rooms where snipping scissors lowered the level of their dresses' bosoms and removed the skirts so as to show bare flesh over stocking tops.

By the time Friday evening came around the saloons' customers were taking bets on how little the girls would be wearing. Kate's girls showed up in low cut outfits which were little more than bodices, for they ended at a level with the brief, frilly-legged panties and left the rest exposed. For her part, Freddie sent the Fair Lady to war wearing skirts that trailed to the floor – at the rear, the entire front being removed to the waist and the upper part cut down to just over the nipples of the girls' unsupported bosoms.

Goggle-eyed cowhands, especially those who came in that day after a month and more on the trail, staggered from one place to the other. The dress of the girls attracted attention from another source too.

"Sarah," Dusty said, entering the main office where his female and male deputies gathered around the desk discussing the saloon feud. "Go tell Freddie I want to see her and for her to come straight away. *In her working clothes!*"

"Sure thing, Cap'n," Sarah replied, noting the emphasis he put on the last four words.

"Lon, go bring Buffalo Kate in. The rest of you get out on your rounds."

When that note entered Dusty Fog's voice, his friends knew better than stand around asking fool questions. At such a moment the best place to be was anywhere well clear of the Rio Hondo gun wizard for, man, he was angry and when Dusty lost his temper it behoved all sensible folks to seek out and take shelter in the storm cellars.

"I'll go change," Freddie said when Sarah brought Dusty's orders.

While she wore her usual working clothes and not the abbreviated costume sported by her girls, Freddie made a point of never visiting anywhere in her capacity as mayor unless dressed town style.

"The Cap'n said to come in your working clothes," Sarah replied.

"But I won't be a moment changing," Freddie objected and started to turn.

Catching Freddie's arm, Sarah held her boss and their

eyes met, surprise showing in the English girl's and grim determination in Sarah's.

"I don't know if I could drag you down there, Miss Freddie," Sarah stated, "but I'll sure as hell have to try. Cap'n Fog's riled and when he's riled it don't pay to go against his orders."

Then Freddie got it. This was not a friendly request from the marshal to the mayor, asking for an informal chat. She was being summoned before the head of the Mulrooney peace officers as a saloon-keeper who had stepped too far over the line. So Freddie went along with Sarah and arrived at the office at the same time as Buffalo Kate appeared escorted by the Kid.

"In here, *ladies*," Dusty ordered, in a tone which showed he did not regard them as being lady-like. "Go help make the round, Sarah, Lon."

Kate glanced at Freddie and promised herself that if the English girl had used her civic influence to make trouble, she would give her the licking of her life on the spot.

If Freddie noticed Kate's expression, she gave no sign of it. On other occasions when Freddie visited Dusty, she found a chair awaiting her. This time there was only one chair and Dusty sat in it, not even bothering to go through the social form of rising when ladies entered the room. For a time nobody spoke. Kate shuffled her feet and even Freddie's serene calm quavered under Dusty's cold-eyed gaze.

"What do they wear on Monday?" he asked at last. "Or aren't you bothering to have them in clothes?"

"That's an idea I hadn't thought of," Freddie said, guessing what was coming and hoping to carry it off lightly. "Although I always believe a girl looks more seductive when wearing just a small amount of clothing."

Her attempt failed by a good country mile.

"Look," Dusty growled. "I don't give a damn that you pair both want to be the saloon queen of Mulrooney. I don't care whose place gets the most trade. What I do care about is you dressing your girls in a way that's hotting up every girl-hungry cowhand, railroad man and skin hunter in town to the point where he's ready to grab hold of the first woman he sees and let it go."

"It's not that bad—" began Kate.

"Like hell it isn't!" Dusty barked. "Three times already tonight I've had to whip down fellers who were all set to go and couldn't find a gal to go with. It's only lucky that I was on hand or some innocent gal would have suffered – and for what, so you pair could try to haul in some of the trade that might be headed to the other's saloon."

"We were only competing for tr—" Freddie started to explain.

"You were acting like a pair of money-hungry sluts without a lousy brain between the pair of you!"

Anger glowed in Freddie's eyes, the kind of righteous anger a guilty conscience faced with the truth often caused.

"You can't talk to *us* like that, Captain Fog!"

"I'll talk to you how I feel like," Dusty answered. "There are men in this town who haven't seen a woman for weeks and you're dangling your half-naked girls all around them. I figured that as mayor, you could be relied on to show better sense than that, *Miss* Woods. And I sure as hell reckoned that you'd been in the saloon business long enough to know better, *Miss* Gilgore. Now get the hell out of my sight, both of you. In thirty minutes I'll be visiting your places and if I find one girl not wearing a dress that comes below the knees all round and covers her tits, I'll close you both down. Got it?"

A red-faced Freddie nodded her head and an equally discomforted Kate gave her silent agreement that she got 'it'. Dusty did not even bother to look at them again. After a significant glance at the wall clock, he settled down to writing in the jail log. Turning, both women slunk out of the office and made their way in silence to the door. In her heart each of them knew Dusty to be right and Freddie could not help but wonder at the change in one whom she always regarded as a quiet-spoken, polite young man.

"Whew!" she gasped as they stepped into the cool night air and the range breeze fanned their hot cheeks. "I feel about three inches high."

"And me," Kate replied. "This was all your fault!"

"Mine!" Freddie squeaked. "You started it when you stole the Pride of Dixie!"

"And you had your sluts stripping on the stage!"

"Don't call my girls sluts. They're not cat-house culls like that bunch you hire."

"Cat-house culls!" Kate hissed, clenching her fists. "You're asking—"

"I make it twenty-three minutes, *ladies!*" Dusty's voice cut in. "You're not giving your girls much time to dress."

For a moment Freddie and Kate glared at each other, standing face to face. Attracted by their voices, a small crowd stood around watching them. Neither wanted to pull out and look like she was running away. Yet neither wanted to have her place closed for disobeying Dusty's orders.

"This town isn't big enough for both of us!" Kate warned. "One of us has got to go!"

"Then you'd better start packing!" Freddie replied. "Good night!"

At exactly the same instant they turned away from each other; Freddie stamping off along the sidewalk and Kate crossing the street. Half an hour Dusty had given them and both knew he would not be more than a few seconds late.

Not until half way to the Buffalo did Kate realize that Freddie had not used her influence to make trouble for her rival, and that Dusty treated his friend – who was also the town's leading citizen – to the same hide-searing tongue-lashing that he dished out to the errant Kate. She was willing to bet that if Freddie failed to improve her girls' dress, the Fair Lady would be padlocked before midnight. So all right, the Limey hadn't screamed out and stood on her civic status; that still did not excuse her insulting Kate's girls. It was time Miss Woods learned who had best claim to the title of saloon queen of Mulrooney.

Freddie stormed back to the Fair Lady, cheeks burning and ears tingling. On the way she decided that she asked for all Dusty said to her, but did not intend to let Kate get away with her insults; Kate was right about one thing; Mulrooney could not hold both of them.

When Dusty arrived at the Fair Lady exactly half an hour after his warning, he found the girls dressed in their original clothes and a much calmer air around the place. On visiting the Buffalo, he saw that Kate had also taken his warning to heart. But he knew the feud was far from over and would not be until one or the other knew for sure who was boss.

A man had been standing outside the jail, down the side alley by Dusty's office and listening to the small Texan's angry words which came through the open window. Just as the listener was about to walk away, he saw a youngster carrying a bundle of large white posters coming along the street. Stopping, the youngster hung one of the posters on a wall, pinning it up with blows of a hammer. Then he came on and halted by the door of the jail.

"Can I put this sign up here, Cap'n?" he called.

Coming from his office, Dusty walked to the front door and looked down at the youngster. "Now that all depends what it is, boy," he said.

"Mr. Dongelon's got him a real fist-fighting ring like they have back east and he's offering a hundred dollars to any feller as can stand up against that pugilist – what in hell that might be – he's brought out from the east."

"Is that so?" Dusty grinned. "When's this pugilist coming?"

"Should be here by Monday, but Mr. Dongelon wants to make sure everybody knows in good time."

"Then you'd best hand up that sign real quick, *amigo*."

The listener remained in the alley until after the boy hung up his sign. After the youngster departed and Dusty had returned to his office, the man left the alley and walked along the street. Finding one of Dongelon's advertising posters on a closed store's wall, the man tore it down and thrust it into his pocket. He went to where a good horse stood, mounted it and rode out of town going west along the railroad track in the direction of Brownton.

Along towards midnight Dusty and the Kid were making their final rounds when they saw a man fastening a poster on to a wall. Neither bothered to check, putting the incident down to some cowhand high-spirits. Most likely he was turning the posters up-side down, or face to the wall; both cowhand tricks when liquored up. It would not harm the posters and might even attract more attention to the forth-coming event Dongelon arranged.

"Let's go grab a cup of coffee, Lon," Dusty said. "Maybe those posters'll take folk's minds off Freddie and Kate."

"Maybe," agreed the Kid.

Freddie Woods was dreaming that she and Buffalo Kate were fighting. They were on the floor, Freddie's right fist dug into the blonde's hair, her left pounding at Kate's face and Babsy stood over them shaking Freddie by the shoulder.

"Miss Freddie! Miss Freddie! Wake up!"

Slowly Freddie came out of her sleep, finding herself lying face down, her right hand gouging into the pillow and her left pounding at it. Standing by the bed and looking excited, Babsy held out a large sheet of white paper with something printed on it. Rolling on to her back, Freddie sat up and pushed her hair out of her eyes. Several of the girls stood behind Babsy and all showed considerable excitement for an early hour on Sunday morning.

"What – what's wro—" Freddie began, then her eyes focused on the poster in Babsy's hands.

CHALLENGE

Miss Freddie Woods and Miss Buffalo Kate Gilgore will engage in a bout of pugilism in the ring at the Buffalo Saloon tonight, Saturday, at 9 o'clock to decide who is the Saloon Queen of Mulrooney, the loser to get out of town and all proceeds to be given to the Mulrooney Church Social Fund.

"Where did you get this?" Freddie gasped.

"Nailed to the wall outside," Babsy replied. "But they're plastered all over town."

Swinging her feet from out of the bed, Freddie rose and crossed the room. She drew back the curtains and looked along Main Street. At three different points, including before the Buffalo Saloon, she saw small groups of excited people standing and looking at sheets of paper nailed to walls.

"Coo'er, Miss Freddie," Babsy said, her eyes wide with surprise. "You never told me you was going to paste her earhole."

"You'll lick her good, Miss Freddie," another of the girls stated and the rest muttered their agreement.

It seemed that the girls took it for granted that Freddie had issued the challenge and all felt assured that she would win. Freddie frowned at the thought. If Kate wanted a fight, and the poster indicated that she did – or why would the poster say the bout's rendezvous was the Buffalo – she could have one. But Freddie wanted the fight to be private. Then Freddie saw the eager faces of her girls and heard their chatter as they excitedly discussed the forthcoming whipping and expulsion of Buffalo Kate.

One thing Freddie knew for certain. Unless she accepted Kate's challenge, she would be finished in Mulrooney.

In the Buffalo, Wally the head bartender stood in Kate's room and watched his boss read the poster he had brought in.

"Are you going through with it, Kate?" he asked.

"Has she left me any choice?" Kate replied. "I'll give her one thing though. She's sport enough to say we'll have the fight here, even if she has given all the profits away."

"Yeah, but—"

"But what?"

"You'll lick her, boss, that's for sure—"

"You don't sound too sure," Kate remarked.

If he had told the truth, Wally was not too sure. Since his arrival in Mulrooney, and despite the feud, Wally had become attached to Vera, one of Freddie's barmaids. Among other things he learned about the talented Miss Woods was how she licked Big Sarah in a fight and, according to Vera, showed considerable fist fighting skill to do so. Wally recalled hearing of women pugilists and had seen one bout between a pair of them. Kate might be a tough girl who could take care of herself in a rough-house barroom brawl, but entering a ring would be a different matter and Wally figured that Miss Woods must expect to have an edge or she would not have selected such a method of settling their differences.

Throwing a poster on the desk in the jail's main office Mark Counter looked at Dusty Fog.

"Do you reckon this'll come off, Dusty?"

"I can't see either of them backing down. With any luck they'll pound some sense into their fool heads and stop this feuding," Dusty replied. "Say, where did you get this?"

"From outside the hotel. It's only one of plenty and they're attracting a heap of interest around town."

Just how much interest became apparent in the next couple of hours. The posters had been spread around town and at the various camps outside city limits. Three trail bosses rode in before eleven to ask if the fight was really on and the whole town buzzed with conjecture. Would the challenge be accepted? If so, who would win?

The good ladies of the town clucked their tongues and shook their heads – possibly because the fight would take place where they could not see it. Of course it was for a good cause, but one hardly expected a for-real lady like Miss Freddie to indulge in such things.

By noon the town had divided itself into two camps and the lawmen were forced to stop three separate fights between members of the two parties – the fights being caused by suggestions that either Freddie or Kate would not dare take up the challenge. When he was called to prevent Shad Birnbaum and Sherill, both members of the Town Council, fighting in the street, Dusty figured it was time somebody knew for sure if the challenge had been taken up. With that in mind, he headed for the Fair Lady and asked if he might see Miss Woods.

"Are you going through with this, Freddie?" he asked, lifting the poster from her bed after being admitted to her room.

"Is Miss Gilgore?" she countered.

"I haven't asked her yet."

"Tell her that I will be willing to drop the matter – if she makes a public announcement that she wants it that way."

"You know damned well that she won't do that!" Dusty barked.

"Then it appears that the challenge is still on."

Much the same took place at the Buffalo, with Kate almost repeating Freddie's words. Yet Dusty gained the impression that neither woman felt entirely happy about the fight. However, neither would be first to back down and so it appeared the fight must still be on.

Dusty passed word around that the challenge had been accepted and the fight would definitely take place. To prevent further disturbances, he also warned that anybody making trouble would be slapped in jail for the night. Such was the eagerness to witness the battle that men leaned over backwards to avoid becoming involved in any trouble which might wind up with them in jail and unable to see it. Never could Dusty remember so quiet and peaceful a Saturday afternoon. Yet to him it seemed like the calm before the storm.

CHAPTER TWELVE

A Drink Before Starting

At a charge of a dollar per head as entrance fee, the Mulrooney Church Social Fund swelled its coffers to a good size; for by half past eight the Buffalo Saloon's big barroom was packed out with almost every man in town. Not only did Dongelon loan and have erected his newly purchased eastern-style ring, but he agreed to act as referee in the bout – which offered him a good view of the entire affair and guaranteed that he got in to see it.

Dusty might have been concerned with who issued the challenge and had the posters put out, but he found himself requested to take charge of the entire affair. The request came from both Freddie and Kate, leaving everything in his hands. Always wishing to nip trouble in the bud, Dusty laid down two rules straight away: first that no liquor would be sold in the saloon; second that neither saloon's girls would be allowed to witness the fight. Feelings ran high among the girls and Dusty knew that having them present might spark off a full-scale riot. Nor would Freddie's girls stay away if Kate's were permitted to attend. So Dusty ruled that neither saloon's girls attended. In doing so he antagonized the entire female staff of two saloons, but hoped that the precaution would be worth it.

There was considerable wagering at even money on the result of the fight, although most of it appeared to be done between individuals rather than with professional gamblers who always preferred to have an edge when betting on anything. Dusty noticed this as he noticed everything else, but did not worry over it. Way he figured things, the trouble would not come until after the fight and he had made arrangements for that.

A considerable noise rose into the air, talk as bets were made or comments thrown around, laughter as somebody made a joke, shuffling and scraping of feet and chairs. Dusty kept his deputies with him at the main doors, all except Big Sarah who had the job of making sure that the Fair Lady girls stayed in their places and the Buffalo's female staff remained at Dongelon's. The noise drowned out any sound that might have come from the street and effectively prevented Dusty hearing certain noises which might have interested him had he heard them.

At nine o'clock a brief, expectant hush fell over the room as Dongelon climbed on to the edge of the raised dais and ducked between the top and center of the three ropes which stretched from corner to corner around it.

"Gentlemen!" he called, waving down the noise. "Your attention, please. Tonight, we are privileged to witness a challenge bout of pugilism—"

"Make it fast and bring on the gals!" whooped a cowhand and a roar of agreement followed his words.

Although Dongelon had thought out quite a speech, there was too much noise for him to finish it. Nor did the noise abate as Buffalo Kate walked from her office and along the narrow aisle leading to the ring. She wore a long cloak which covered her from her neck to her bare feet; and Wally followed carrying a bucket and bottle full of water and a couple of towels. On reaching the ring, Kate climbed up the steps and ducked between the ropes, walking to the corner Dongelon pointed out as being her own. There she removed her cloak and passed it to Wally. The crowd showed its appreciation for she wore a brief chemise that showed off a plump but shapely figure.

Even as Kate removed her robe, Freddie entered the ring followed by Vera as her second. Freddie removed her cloak and various male eyes stuck out like organ-stops at what they saw. Under the cloak Freddie wore an outfit consisting of a pair of black tights and a candy-striped upper section that looked like a man's sleeveless vest – although it was not a man's figure inside the vest.

After a moment the men forgot their admiration of Freddie's magnificent body and started studying her as a contestant who either stood to win or lose them some money. While Kate looked a mite taller and some heavier, Freddie did not give the impression of being puny. Fact being, she looked like a tolerable strong gal and more than one member of the crowd recalled how she knocked cold a drunken railroad man with one punch when he tried to paw her at the Fair Lady. One thing was for sure, everybody in the crowd figured, whichever way things went they were in for seeing a helluva fight.

"How about a drink before you start, ladies?" Wally asked.

"Good idea," Kate replied for she had never felt more like taking a drink.

"Certainly," Freddie agreed, feeling much the same way.

Leaving the ring, Wally hurried back to the office and returned carrying a tray with three glasses of whisky on it. Vera took two of the glasses from him and passed them to Freddie and Kate while Dongelon collected the third.

"Here's to your health, while you still have it," Freddie said, raising her glass and smiling at Kate with more confidence than she felt.

Grinning, Kate replied, "Here's looking at you, while you can still see me."

Then both of them tossed off their drinks in a single gulp, much to the relief of two of the watching crowd. The glasses were removed from the ring and Dongelon handed Freddie and Kate two Indian-pennies each. They were to hold a coin in the palm of each hand, keeping the fist clenched and preventing the fight developing into a hair-yanking brawl. Quickly Dongelon told the girls the rules, for the crowd were growing rowdily restless and he wanted to start the fight.

Freddie felt sleepy as she walked forward to toe the line painted across the center of the ring. However, she kept her fists up and as soon as she came into range cut loose with a left and a right that set Kate back on her heels. Following up the blows, Freddie walked into a punch thrown by Kate. It crashed against her cheek and sent her staggering back to the ropes. For a moment Freddie hung on the ropes. She felt puzzled as she shook her head. While the blow landed with a fair amount of power behind it, she should not feel so dizzy. For some reason Kate did not follow up her advantage. Instead of moving in and landing more blows, the blonde stood in the ring center and rocked her head from side to side as if to clear it.

Giving a yawn, Freddie moved forward but although her brain knew what to do it failed to communicate the orders correctly to her hands. Closing with Kate, she swung a fist into the blonde's ribs and felt a blow in her side, yet it lacked power. Drowsiness clouded over Freddie and she tried to shake it off, clinging to Kate. Instead of thrusting Freddie away, Kate let the coins drop from her hands and locked her arms around the other girl's waist. Ominous growls and calls rose from the crowd and Dongelon tried to separate the girls. In a way he succeeded, for he got them apart. Then their legs buckled under them and they slid to the floor of the ring, rolling on to their backs and lying still.

A sudden silence, brought about by surprise at the

sight of both girls collapsing, dropped over the room. Outside sounded a dull, muffled boom; like when a hard-rock miner touched off an explosive charge underground. If the crowd had been maintaining their noise, the sound of the boom might have gone unnoticed. As it was Dusty heard, so did his deputies and their eyes turned to him.

"That was down by the bank!" the Kid stated.

"Let's go!" Dusty replied.

Even as the five lawmen dashed from the saloon, a man yelled that the fight was a fake rigged by Freddie. Instantly one of Freddie's supporters jumped up and swung a punch. Like ripples raised by a stone thrown into a lake, the brawl spread across the room as furious men deprived of what they hoped would be a damned good fight began to vent their annoyance on each other. Not only the cowhands and other workers were involved, but the upper-classes, including the banker and most of the town council became involved in the general brawl.

In the ring Dongelon stared down at the two still shapes at his feet. Then he turned and glared at Wally for he had seen knock-out drops in action often enough to recognize their effects when he saw them. What Dongelon could not understand was why Wally slipped his boss the drops as well as dosing Freddie.

"What happened?" he growled as the bartender came to his side.

"Me 'n Vera reckoned a draw'd maybe satisfy the bosses, We don't want to see either of 'em run out of town," Wally replied.

"Very noble!" growled Dongelon, ducking as a chair flew through the air. "Now how do we get out of here?"

Looking at the fighting mass of men around the ring, Wally grinned and replied, "I reckon we're safer right here."

"Could be at that!" Dongelon admitted, stepping to the ropes and laying his hand on a man's face to shove him backwards as he tried to climb through the ropes.

The battle raged on, with Dongelon, Wally and Vera holding back the fighters and preventing any entering the ring to disturb the rest of the two women who ought to have been indulging in a bout of pugilism but instead lay on their backs and slept like two innocent babes. Not even the crackle of gun-fire from outside and along the street brought an end to the fight.

Dusty and his men ran along the street and the big shape of his female deputy loomed up ahead of them. Coming forward, she pointed to the bank.

"You hear it, Dusty?" she asked, dropping the formal "Cap'n" in her excitement and concern.

"We're on our way, Sarah-gal," Dusty replied.

"How about that bunch at the saloon?" she went on as a man came flying through one of the windows in a shower of glass.

"Let 'em fight. The bank's a whole sight more important right now."

Which, bitter as the thought might have been to Buffalo Kate as owner – had she been able to hear it – was the living truth. The bank held thousands of dollars; money to purchase cattle or buffalo hides and tongues from the men who brought them, the herd price left in safekeeping by three trail bosses while they enjoyed the pleasures of Mulrooney, and the savings of most of the folks in town. If the contents of the bank's safe were stolen, the result would be bankruptcy and ruin for most of the town.

A grin crossed Sarah's face as she took the point and a thought struck her.

"Go get 'em boys!" she whooped and dashed off in the direction of the Fair Lady, traveling at a fair speed considering her bulky build.

Dusty and the deputies had more to occupy their

minds than thinking about Sarah's apparent desertion.
If any of them thought about the matter at all, they put
it down to her going to fetch a gun from the jail and not
to cowardice.

In this they were wrong. Big Sarah knew her
limitations and usefulness as a deputy. Handling female
miscreants was her work, getting tangled in gunfights
had no part in her duties. While she could handle a
shotgun with reasonable skill, she reckoned her limited
talents would not be needed in that field; fact being that
she could even get in her friend's way at a time when
they needed to be free agents if they hoped to stay alive.
So she let the men handle men's work and decided to
make a stab at stopping the brawl at the Buffalo.

There was one chance of her doing it. Mulrooney's
fire brigade, like most western towns, was manned by
volunteers and most of the men were at the saloon.
However, the two fire engines stood in their house and
were of a pattern requiring only a limited knowledge to
handle them. Sarah reckoned that she and the girls of
the Fair Lady could haul one of the engines down and
manage to make it work long enough for their purposes.

Throwing open the batwing doors of the Fair Lady,
Sarah looked in at the morose girls who sat around.
Practically the full working strength of the saloon sat in
the barroom, more than enough to achieve Sarah's purpose.

"Miss Freddie's in trouble!" she yelled.

Instantly the lethargy dropped from the girls and
Babsy sprang to her feet. "Let's do them Buffalo
bitches!" she screeched.

"Hold it!" Sarah bellowed. "It's not them. There's a
riot at the Buffalo. We're going to borrow a fire engine
and damp 'em down a mite."

With eager squeals the girls dashed from the saloon,
grateful for a chance to relieve their boredom, and went
streaming off in the direction of the firehouse. The

cracking of shots behind the jail slowed them, but Sarah urged them on, telling them that Cap'n Fog was handling things.

Just as she led the girls towards the firehouse, Sarah remembered there were two engines in it. Leaving the other girls to go alone she headed for the Wooden Spoon and met the hostile stares of Kate's girls who had come out to see what caused all the shouting and noise.

"Your boss needs help!" Sarah announced.

"Come on, girls!" Ginger yelled. "I knew we shouldn't trust those—"

"It's not the Fair Lady girls, it's a riot at the Buffalo," Sarah interrupted. "Fair Lady's gone for a fire engine to help stop it."

Sarah relied on the "anything Fair Lady can do, we can do a whole heap better" attitude of the Buffalo girls to gain her the required support and she proved correct.

"Come on, girls!" howled a big, buxom brunette, "let's show them Fair Lady cows how Buffalo can move."

Two swarms of girls descended on the firehouse where the two hand-drawn fire engines stood ready for use, big water tanks full and the wheels coated in antelope grease for easy rolling. All thoughts of settling their private differences by hand-scalpings had been forgotten, although the rivalry remained. Eager hands grabbed the towing handles of both engines, plump bare shoulders rested against the rear to add motive power by pushing. Sheer weight of numbers started the two engines running at almost the same instant; the Buffalo girls, having a shorter distance to run, arrived at the same moment as the Fair Lady's group and both saloon contingents went to it with a will and eagerness to show the other who was best.

Babsy grabbed hold of the speaking trumpet which hung on the side of the Fair Lady's engine and without asking for permission appointed herself commander of her saloon's machine. In a voice that was squeaky with excitement, she began to exhort her saloon to pull and show those flabby old hags next door what *young* ladies could do.

After throwing an angry glance at Babsy, Ginger released her hold of the Buffalo engine's towing handle and grabbed their speaking trumpet. She began to screech encouragement to the Buffalo girls, telling them to show that fat blonde foreigner and those worn out old hags what a good saloon's girls could manage.

Ignoring the sporadic bursts of shooting which wafted to their ears, the girls dragged their engines from the firehouse down on Main Street and brought them to a halt facing the shattered windows of the Buffalo Saloon. Inside the battle still raged in all its fury and from the sound of breaking furniture Buffalo Kate would have little left for her customers to sit upon when she next opened.

Quickly the girls followed the pattern they had often seen used by the town's volunteer firemen. In the slack days, while waiting for trade to come to Mulrooney, watching the fire crews in training had formed a welcome break from the dull, customerless hours in the Fair Lady and Freddie's girls knew the drill very well. However, the engines had been designed for simplicity in operation so that poorly trained and unhandy crews would be able to handle them in an emergency, so the Buffalo girls had little difficulty in preparing their outfit for operation. A buxom, strong girl uncoiled each hose and headed towards the windows with the self-appointed engine commanders at their sides and screeching demands that the other members of the crew got water coming. Girls grabbed the pump handles on either side of the engines and others caught up the buckets, forming a chain to the filled waterbarrels on the edge of the sidewalk, ready to refill the engines' tanks.

"Go to it, girls!" Sarah yelled. "Pump!"

A big, burly man reeled through the batwing doors of

the saloon, his shirt torn off and his mouth bleeding. From all appearances he looked too wild to care who he attacked as long as he attacked somebody, so Sarah took no chances. Folding her right hand, she swung it to crash against the man's thrust-out jaw and sent him backwards into the saloon where he fell onto his back and lost all further interest in the proceedings.

Down went the pump handle at one side and up rose the other side, to be thrust downwards again by eager arms. The two girls holding the hoses felt a stirring, swelling pulsation as water was forced through the canvas and held at the closed nozzles just waiting to burst out when the taps opened.

"Now!" Sarah roared.

Turning on the nozzle taps, the two girls released their jets of water. The hose could throw a jet one hundred and fifty feet into the air when given the full power of the pumps behind them. Even with the slightly less than full force the girls managed, the water flew out at a tolerable rate and when it landed packed a considerable amount of power. The twin jets sprang forward through the windows and swept among the fighting crowd, felling men like ninepins, knocking breath and aggressive desires out of fighting bodies.

The effort at stopping the brawl would not be made without sacrifices. Sweat poured down faces, washing away make-up; hair came down and straggled untidily; suspender straps popped and runs developed in stockings or, freed of their restraint, the stockings slid down; shoes were lost, dresses splashed and soaked in water; yet the girls ignored all those minor inconveniences in their efforts to end the fight.

Babsy and Ginger were yelling themselves hoarse as they urged their girls to better efforts and pointed out promising targets to the hose-handlers. Of course, it *was* only coincidence when Babsy screeched:

"There, that ginger-haired bloke!"

Obligingly the Fair Lady's hose-handler swung her nozzle in the required direction and swept a red-headed buffalo hunter from his feet just as he was about to fell a cowhand from behind and using a legless chair.

"Get that fat blond jasper!" Ginger yelled after scanning the crowd to pick a likely target and again the color of the hair *was* mere coincidence.

Flicking an annoyed glance at Ginger, Babsy directed the jet to where Banker Coutland and Mr. Sherill were settling an ancient difference of opinion in a most satisfactory and enjoyable manner. Sherill held the post as Fire Chief and it struck Babsy as being apt that he should learn how effective his fire engines' hoses could be.

Roaring with rage, a man tried to climb out of the window but Babsy's hose-handler washed him back inside like a log caught in a flash-flood. Then Babsy saw a cowhand coming through the batwing doors and directed the hose at him. In doing so, completely by accident? she managed to have Ginger drenched in the side-spray from the jet. Even if that was an accident, the same could not be said for Ginger's action in grabbing a bucket full of water from one of her girls and heaving its contents over a second man who tried to get out of the door, but included Babsy very generously in its wash.

Dropping her speaking trumpet, Babsy swung towards Ginger and the little redhead let the bucket fall. Before they reached each other, a hand caught each girl by the scruff of her neck.

"Start anything and I'll crack your heads together!" Big Sarah warned.

Being sensible girls, even if a mite hot-tempered, and having a marked aversion to getting their heads cracked together, Babsy and Ginger decided to postpone hostilities until a later and more convenient moment. Confining themselves to nothing more than poking their tongues out at each other, the two girls went back to controlling their hose-handler's fire and picking off likely targets in the crowd.

By the time the water barrels were empty and the pumps sucking the last drops out of the engine's tanks, all resistance ended in the saloon. Limp, soaking and winded men no longer felt any desire to fight, but Sarah found her troubles had not ended.

The exhausted girls leaned on the hitching rails or sagged against pump handles. All but Babsy and Ginger. Although soaked to the skin and hoarse from giving encouragement to their friends, neither had been through so great an exertion as the pump crews or bucket lines.

"I bet Freddie Woods started that so she wouldn't get licked!" Ginger said.

"Miss Freddie doesn't need help to lick a fat bladder like Buffalo Kate!" Babsy croaked back. "Buffalo's a good name for her, she looks like one."

"Don't you talk about Kate like that!"

"Or what'll you do?"

Instantly both groups of girls tensed, forgetting their tiredness and remembering their feud. Sarah knew she must act fast or wind up with another riot on her hands, one she might not stop so easily. However, Sarah was a woman and understood the working of a female mind.

"You girls sure look a sight," she said. "Won't the townswomen laugh when they arrive?"

Every girl stopped in her tracks, staring at the bedraggled condition of the opposing group, then the girls around her. Not one of them wished to have anybody, much less the good ladies of the town, see them in that state. Forgetting their disagreements, deserting the pumps and leaving shoes behind them, the Fair Lady girls dashed back to the shelter of their saloon and the Buffalo contingent fled to the rear of the building to use the back door and get out of sight.

With a grin, Sarah leaned on the hitching rail and

watched the soaking men limp out of the saloon. Most
of them carried some sign of being involved in the fight
and she figured Dusty would be able to round them up
in the morning. Then she wondered where Dusty and
the others might be for she could not remember hearing
any shooting for several minutes.

CHAPTER THIRTEEN

The Wisdom of Buying a Sharps

Dusty and his deputies raced along the street after leaving Big Sarah. In passing the bank they wasted no time stopping to peer through the windows. The safe had been built, literally, into the rear office where Coutland sat in his glory during business hours, and could not be seen from Main Street. On taking over his duties as marshal, Dusty had commented on the inadvisability of such an arrangement. However, Coutland claimed his safe could stand up to the attentions of any thief and that it would take a fair charge of explosive to force its doors – and a fair charge of explosive made enough noise to attract attention, especially at night when the only chance of forcing the door would be presented. Anyway, removing the safe and placing it in the front office could only be done by almost destroying and then rebuilding the bank, so Coutland felt reluctant to make the effort and Dusty, thinking on the same lines as the banker where the noise of safe-blowing was concerned, did not press the demand. Now it seemed that somebody had taken advantage of the weakness in the bank's defenses and picked a real good night to make the effort. If the two girls had not collapsed at that time, most likely the crowd would have been making so much noise that the muffled boom of the explosion could not be heard by anybody in the saloon.

Fanning out and drawing their guns, Dusty's party split into two groups, Mark, Derringer and Waco going down the right of the bank while Dusty and the Kid went along the left, making for the rear of the building.

"It's the law!" a voice yelled and a tall, dark shape loomed up in the darkness at the rear of the building.

Flame spurted from the dark shape and Frank Derringer gave a pain-fulled curse as lead sliced along his neck, giving him a nasty graze and the best piece of good luck a professional gambling man could have asked for. An inch to the left and Derringer would have been lying on the ground, blood pumping from a hole in the tender part of his favorite throat.

Mark and Waco fired on the run, their two guns roaring out at almost the same instant. Caught by the two .44 caliber bullets, the shape went backwards, its gun sending a shot into the ground as it fell from a lifeless hand. Three of them in the alley made too large a target for either Mark or Waco to take a chance on anything other than shooting to kill.

"You all right, Frank?" Waco asked. "I'm not worried, only there's some things you haven't taught me yet."

"Thanks for the concern, boy," Derringer answered, touching his neck with a delicate finger tip. "It's only a nick."

Feet thudded and voices spat out curses behind the building. Always eager to get into action, and not yet having learned wisdom and caution, Waco sprang forward. Before he reached the corner, a big hand clamped on his shoulder and jerked him back. Mark accomplished the feat without releasing his Colt, for his left arm was still in the sling although fast recovering from its wound.

"Try thinking, boy," he growled in the youngster's ear. "They know we're at this end and are watching for us."

Subsequent events proved that Mark called the

situation one hundred percent correctly. Three men who had burst out of the bank, all holding short-barrelled guns of cheap and fairly reliable manufacture and known as Suicide Specials, gave their full attention to the left side of the building and ignored the right. Which showed a lamentable lack of foresight on their part, but they were city men and regarded all westerners as dumb, half-witted yokel hicks.

"Law here!" Dusty snapped as he and the Kid came into sight at the other end of the building. "Drop the guns."

Having heard the shooting at the other end, Dusty and the Kid figured that the men from the building might be concentrating in that direction. Their figuring proved correct, but the three men whirled around fast at Dusty's challenge and when they turned, they – in the western phrase – turned shooting. In that they made a damned bad mistake for they were city men more used to knuckle-duster or knife than to handling firearms; and a city father never sired a criminal son who could match a Texas cowhand in the skilled and fast handling of a gun.

Dusty's Colts bellowed and once again his ambidextrous skill showed to its best advantage as the right hand revolver tumbled one of the trio over backwards while the left side gun planted lead into the second man's shoulder. With lead singing around his ears from fast-triggered but poorly-aimed shots fired by the trio, the Kid fired hip-high and by instinctive alignment. Instinctive or taken from a bench rest the Kid reckoned to be able to call his shots with better than fair accuracy at such a moment. He showed his skill by sending a flat-nosed .44 Henry bullet into the remaining member of the trio's chest and spinning the man over like he had been struck by a charging buffalo.

Silence dropped after the flurry of shots, only the noise of the saloon brawl in the background breaking it. Mark called for permission to come out of the alley,

taking an elementary precaution. Way he saw it, the less
chances a lawman took at such a moment, the better his
expectancy of living long enough to retire and spend his
old age hard-wintering* around the general store's
stove.

"D – don't shoot!" croaked one of the wounded
men. "I'm d—"

"Shut it!" growled the Kid, his voice Comanche-
mean.

Even more than Derringer, the three Texans noticed
how the Kid stood. He looked like a blue-tick hound hit-
ting hot cougar scent, or trying to catch some faint
sound of a long-traveling pack baying.

"What's up, Lon?" asked Waco.

"There's another one out that ways," the Kid replied,
pointing unerringly off into the darkness.

"Go get him!" Dusty ordered.

"Su – Damn it, he's took to a hoss."

Luck favored the Texas lawmen that night; or maybe
it was old *Ka-dih*, the Great Spirit of the Comanche
favoring his quarter-blood follower. Whatever the
reason, the Kid had left his big white stallion in the
livery barn's open corral that night instead of using a
stall indoors.

Twice the Kid's piercing whistle rang through the
night. In the corral, the seventeen hand horse threw
back its head, snorted and started running for the fence.
It took off and sailed over that six foot high man-made
barrier like a frog hopping over a hickory twig, lighting
down and racing through the night to answer its
master's summons.

Bounding afork the big white, the Kid headed it
across the range, making after the escaping member of
the gang. Dusty watched his Indian-dark young friend
go, then gave his orders.

---

* Hard-wintering: Old-timers' habit of discussing the hard winters
they *had* lived through.

"Mark, Frank, stay here. Waco, let's go get the horses."

It was an ideal arrangement. With his arm in a sling, Mark could not handle a hard-riding chase through the night and Derringer did not own a personal mount. So they stayed guarding the prisoner while Dusty and the youngster headed for the livery barn.

"It sounds like they're still having fun at the Buffalo, Mark," Derringer said as he collected the gang's weapons.

"Sounds that way," Mark agreed. "Watch 'em while I go in and light a lamp. We'll corral 'em in the office while you go fetch the doctor."

On lighting the lamp, Mark discovered that Coutland's faith in the safe had not been misplaced, for the explosion did not appear to have opened the door. He wasted no time in idle thoughts, but ordered the wounded men who could to come inside while Derringer brought the other in. Then Derringer left to collect the doctor and hoped that his trip would not be wasted due to the doctor being at the Buffalo Saloon. Derringer kept to the rear of Main Street and so did not see the effective way Big Sarah quelled the riot. Finding the doctor at home, Derringer asked for help and the two men returned to the bank.

The Kid allowed his big white stallion to follow the sound of the departing rider. For two miles the stallion covered ground at a fast lope, closing the distance with the other man's mount for there were few horses in the West to equal the Kid's in a chase.

Out on the range, the moon's light gave better visibility than in town and the Kid saw the other rider ahead of him, going down a slope towards the open floor of a valley bottom. The rider was a tall man wearing range clothes and sitting his horse with more skill than a town-bred criminal would be likely to learn.

For a moment the Kid figured maybe his senses, or the white's ability to trail by sound, had gone back on him. That feller down there did not belong to a gang of city owlhoots. Of course he might be a chance traveler who heard the shooting back by town and figured to stay clear of flying lead.

Then the man answered the Kid's doubts in an unmistakable manner. Just as he reached the foot of the slope, the man chanced to look back and saw the tall, black-dressed shape following him. Instantly the man bent forward, jerked out his rifle, twisted in the saddle as he raised it, and fired two shots upwards. Turning forward again, the man urged his horse at a better speed across the quarter of a mile wide bottom of the valley. Out in the center of the valley rose a large rocky outcrop and the man had passed it when he turned and saw the Kid ignoring his warning. Once more the rifle began to spit flame.

Three shots whined by the Kid's head and when the fourth sent his Stetson flying, he decided the time had come to show his disapproval. At a heel-touch the white stallion made better speed and the "yellow boy" flowed to the Kid's shoulder. Twice the Kid's rifle cracked, but firing from the back of a running horse – especially when riding without a saddle or even blanket – had never been conducive to extreme accuracy. Instead of tumbling the man from his saddle, one bullet missed and the other ripped into his horse's rump and brought the animal down.

"Now I've got him!" thought the Kid.

Only it seemed that old *Ka-Dih* reckoned he had done enough for Long Walker's grandson that night. The rider had passed the outcrop where he might have taken cover and was within thirty yards of the valley's other slope when his horse went down. To make things worse, some damned fool had built a dugout home on the slope ahead of the man: a dugout being a temporary dwelling built by digging a rectangular pit into a convenient slope, erecting a wooden and sod framework and packing the excavated dirt around and on the roof of the frame, putting a door in the front wall but managing without the luxury of windows.

Before the Kid could zero in his rifle on him, the running man plunged through the open door and out of sight. Instantly the Kid forgot about shooting and headed his stallion for the cover of the outcrop. He was barely in time, for a bullet stirred his hair in passing as he reined his horse behind the outcrop. Dropping from the white's back, the Kid moved to where he could see and shoot at the door of the dugout, throwing a couple of shots across the two hundred odd yards. He had little hope of making a hit but reckoned he could show the man inside that he was still around.

"Well," thought the Kid, looking at the dugout, "you can't get out of there, *hombre* – but we'll have a helluva time getting in."

With which view Dusty Fog agreed on his arrival. He and Waco halted their paint stallions on top of the slope and waited until the Kid gave them covering fire before riding down to join him. Studying the situation, Dusty noted the thickness of the roof of the dugout and the lack of cover between its door and the outcrop. To try rushing the building would be certain death if the man inside proved to be resolute and anything like a rifle shot.

"All right, *hombre!*" Dusty called. "This's the marshal of Mulrooney. Come on out with your hands raised."

"You got no jurisdiction out here!" the man replied and Dusty had a feeling he should recognize the voice.

"I'm a deputy sheriff, too," Dusty answered. "This's still in the county. Come on and you'll not get hurt."

"Try coming to get me and you will!" the man yelled defiantly.

"Man'd say he's got a right good point there, Dusty," drawled the Kid.

"Could maybe sneak around, get on top of the dugout and shoot down," Waco suggested.

"Sure, if you knew for sure where the feller was, and he didn't hear you on top. Because, boy, if you missed or he heard you, he'd start pumping lead right up through the roof."

"Which wouldn't suit Babsy one lil mite, boy," the Kid continued from where Dusty left off. "If he shot you there how could you—"

Waco's interruption was blistering, coarse and profane. "Anybody'd think there was something 'tween Babsy and me," he finished.

"Now what gave you that idea, boy?" grinned the Kid.

While this went on, Dusty had been surveying the surrounding area in the hope of finding something to break the deadlock. At last he made his decision. The man wanted to play mean, so all right, Dusty aimed to play the game the way that jasper called it.

"Go back to town, Lon," he ordered. "Take our hosses back over the slope – no, best leave them here, they're safe. Head back and bring the Sharps."

"Like that, huh?" asked the Kid.

"Just like that," Dusty agreed, his voice as cold and emotionless as a judge pronouncing the death sentence.

After the Kid rode off, Waco sat with his back to a rock and his fingers drumming on the butt of his rifle as he sank deep into thought. Dusty watched the dugout's door and let the youngster continue thinking, guessing the lines Waco's thought-train followed.

"Those fellers'd've been *loco* to try blowing out the safe happen near on every man in town hadn't been at the Buffalo and making a helluva noise," Waco finally stated.

"You figured that too, boy?"

"Sounds like sense. Happen things hadn't quietened down when they did, we might never have heard her blow."

"Right as the off-side of a horse," Dusty admitted. "If the girls hadn't wound up sleeping – sleeping! How the hell did that happen? They hadn't knocked each other cold.''

"Dunno," Waco answered. "I figured they'd go at least half an hour.''

"So did I. Freddie's fit and tough and so's Kate or I miss my guess. And the crowd would have been making plenty of noise all the time. Wouldn't be many of them leaving the saloon right after the fight either, especially when the bar opened. It can't be a coincidence that the gang just happened to hit tonight.''

"You reckon the fight was rigged so they – Hell, Dusty, Miss Freddie nor Buffalo Kate wouldn't do nothing like that.''

"Which same brings up another point," Dusty said, "Who tossed out the challenge and got them together? I got the feeling that neither of the girls had thrown it. Freddie wouldn't and Kate'd prefer to chance her luck in a barroom brawl not a boxing ring – Hey though, that cowhand Lon and I saw last night. Maybe he wasn't fooling with the posters Dongelon put up, but was hanging the challenge signs up for folks to read in the morning.''

"In cahoots with the owlhoots?''

"Or hired without knowing a thing. Those fellers knew their work, boy, they weren't yearling beef. Either them, or somebody local, saw a chance in the feud, knew neither Freddie nor Kate could, or would, back down and fixed the challenge to get the menfolks off the streets and cover the noise of blowing the safe.''

"You mean somebody in town set it up?" Waco growled.

"Boy, a good rule for a lawman to follow is never name names until he's got enough evidence to take before a judge. I've my suspicions, but they're staying mine until I'm sure of them. Now settle down, we've a long wait until dawn.''

The night dragged by. An hour passed before the Kid returned, coming in on foot to bring word of how Big

Sarah quelled the saloon riot. Then he glided back up the slope once more and it is doubtful if the man in the dugout ever knew of the visit.

At dawn, Dusty and Waco prepared their horses for riding and by the time they finished the sun had lit the whole floor of the valley, showing the door of the dugout clearly.

"You in there!" Dusty called, thrusting his carbine into its saddleboot. "Come out with your hands raised!"

"Go to hell!"

"This's your last chance. Come out or we'll fetch you out."

"So come and try it!" screeched the man and fired two shots at the rocks.

To do so he had to expose the barrel of his rifle and part of his body around the side of the door. Which was what Dusty had been waiting for. The small Texan raised his hand and waved it towards the dugout.

A quarter of a mile away the Ysabel Kid sat on the opposite slope to the dugout. He held a Sharps Old Reliable rifle cradled at his shoulder, its barrel further supported by a Y-shaped stick which had been thrust into the ground. For days the Kid had been burning the Mulrooney taxpayers' good powder and shot learning how the big rifle held at various long ranges, so as to be ready to handle such a situation. This was the kind of conditions Dusty envisaged when suggesting the purchase of the rifle as part of the office armament. The wisdom of buying a Sharps proved itself at that moment.

Eagle-keen eyes located the hidden man and sighted the rifle. The Kid heard Dusty's warnings, the replies and the two shots. Then he squeezed the Sharp's trigger. All was ready as he did so; the sights erected and laid with care, a cigar-long cartridge in the chamber, one hundred and twenty grains of prime du Pont powder set to expel a .45 caliber, five hundred and fifty grain bullet through the barrel. The gun's hammer fell and it roared loud in the still of the morning. With the instinct of a good shot, the Kid knew he held true and a scream of pain confirmed his knowledge.

The instant the shot roared out Dusty and Waco sprang into action. They hit their saddles and shot one from either side of the outcrop, heading for the dugout and hanging over the outer flank of their horses like a brace of Comanche bucks. Converging on the dugout, they dropped from their horses, drawing their guns as they landed and dived through the door. The guns were not needed. Hit in the shoulder, moaning in agony and helpless through shock, Vince Crocker, the Brownton deputy marshall was in no shape to make further trouble.

CHAPTER FOURTEEN

Showdown for Two

"Banks Fagan fixed the whole deal," Crocker moaned, looking at the men who stood alongside his bed and conscious that his words were being taken down by the banker's secretary. "He knew those city boys and brought them in for it."

The time was shortly after nine on Sunday morning and Crocker lay on a cell bunk in the Mulrooney jail, his shoulder swathed in bandages, feeling eagerness to lighten his own load by incriminating his boss. Dusty, Mark, Coutland, the local justice of the peace and the banker's secretary stood in the cell to hear Crocker's confession. Both the judge and Coutland showed visible signs of having been at the Buffalo the previous night and having taken part in the brawl.

"Who rigged the challenge between Miss Woods and Miss Gilgore?" Dusty asked.

"Banks. Him and the mayor's been looking for a way to wreck Mulrooney and Banks thought up the idea of having the bank robbed. Only he aimed to get rid of the gang and split the money two ways with me. He knew that fuss between Kate and the Woods dame would blow wide open and when his scout brought Dongelon's sign, he saw his chance. He had contacted the city gang and they were ready to move. So he had the Brownton printer run off those signs and spread them round town. Knew neither dame'd back down and figgered the noise'd last long enough for the gang to do their work. I was to watch 'em and make sure they brought him the money, then we aimed to gun them down and split the take two ways.''

"Got that, ma'am?" Dusty asked the secretary.

"Yes."

"Have him put his mark on the statement, How's about it, Judge?"

"Brownton's not in your jurisdiction, Captain Fog," the Judge replied.

"Not as marshal, but as deputy sheriff it is," Dusty told him.

"Then I'll go make out the warrant for Fagan's arrest. Can you serve it?"

"I reckon we'll give it a try," Dusty said quietly. "There's another thing, Judge."

"And that is?"

"The riot at the Buffalo last night. I reckon five dollars a man might just about compensate Miss Gilgore for the damage."

"That's reasonable," agreed the judge.

"Then I'll start with you and Mr. Coutland, or did you get that lip from walking into a door?"

For a moment the judge spluttered, then he gave a laugh and dipped his hand into his pocket. "Come on, Coutland," he said. "Pay your fine like a good citizen."

"All right," Coutland replied. "How about the others, Captain Fog?"

"I'll get round to them, don't you worry about that," Dusty promised.

While awaiting the arrival of the warrant, Dusty found he had another problem dropped into his lap. Big Sarah arrived, looking like she brought bad news – which she did.

"It's Miss Freddie and Buffalo Kate," she said.

"What about them now?" Dusty groaned, although he could have guessed.

"Kate sent word across that she's coming for a showdown at ten o'clock, and she aims to run Miss Freddie out of town."

"That figures," Dusty grunted. "The damned fool women. I've enough on my hands right now without those two starting again. I can't stay in town. If I don't take Fagan soon, he'll get to hear we captured his boys and'll put out."

"Somebody's got to ask a fool question," Mark drawled. "Might as well be me. Why not tell Freddie and Kate to forget it?"

"That's a fool question all right," grinned Big Sarah. "Those two gals'll never rest easy until they know who's boss; and they'll have this whole town split down the middle siding one or the other before a week's out. Let's leave 'em settle it this morning. I reckon I can keep it off the streets."

Recalling the efficient manner in which Sarah coped with the riot at the Buffalo, Dusty grinned and nodded. "I reckon you can at that. Mark'll be here at the jail—"

"And happen he's any sense, he'll stay here. This's woman's work and too dangerous for a man."

Mark remembered the battle at Bearcat Annie's place in Quiet Town, where only nine women had been involved, and felt inclined to agree with Sarah.

Ten minutes later the warrant for Banks Fagan's arrest arrived. Dusty, Waco, the Kid and Derringer checked their guns then went to collect their horses. In the office Mark sat down to write up the log and Sarah put her badge on straight, winked at him and left the building making for the Fair Lady.

One thing was for sure, Freddie did not intend avoiding a clash but aimed to avoid too much damage to her place. Already the girls had removed the chandelier and packed away all the glassware, covered the bar mirror with wooden boards and fitted shutters across the inside of the windows that overlooked Main Street. In the center of the barroom Freddie, dressed as on the previous night, stopped directing the final preparations and nodded a greeting to Sarah.

"I'm sorry you won't be in on this, Sarah," she said. "Can I do anything for you?"

"Sure, give me the key to the front doors and line the girls up for a search."

"Is that necessary?" Freddie smiled. "This is between Kate and I."

"Likely," Sarah said dryly. "Only I aim to search Buffalo and I don't play any favorites."

It was an argument Freddie could well understand. She gave the order and her girls formed a line along which Sarah went, patting over each girl in turn to make sure no lethal weapons were carried. To further lessen the chances of serious injury Sarah ordered the removal of rings and bracelets, dropping them into a buckskin bag she brought for the purpose. At the end of the search, she accepted the front doors' key from Freddie and left the saloon.

On her arrival at the Buffalo, Sarah met with a cool reception until Kate arrived. The big blonde saloonkeeper wore a man's shirt, jeans and moccasins and like Freddie had no jewelery on. Kate gave the order which allowed Sarah to search and disarm the Buffalo girls, trusting the female deputy's word that Fair Lady had been given the same treatment.

Five minutes after the search, Sarah watched the Buffalo girls troop into the Fair Lady and locked the doors behind them. Just as she turned from the door, Sarah found a procession descending on her. Led by Lily Gouch, the staff of the brothel came towards the saloon.

"I just heard and figger to help Miss Freddie," the madam stated.

"They're about even numbered," Sarah replied. "If you want to help Freddie, send your gals back to the house and have them start tearing up bandages."

For a moment Lily Gouch stood undecided. Then she

gave a shrug. She had seen enough of Sarah in her official capacity as deputy to know the girl could be trusted, so turned and gave the order to her girls.

"How about me?" Lily asked as the girls departed.

"Sun's warm," Sarah replied, ignoring a crash and yells from inside the saloon. "Why not sit on the porch across there with me and we'll wait until the noise dies down before we open the doors."

"You've got a good idea there," Lily answered. "I reckon we might have a tolerable long wait."

And Lily proved to be right.

Kate and Freddie faced each other, each with her girls standing in a watchful half circle behind her. One look told Freddie that Kate came to fight, although she never doubted that. Kate felt just as sure that Freddie did not put on that outfit because she aimed to back down and run.

"This's between you and me," Kate said.

"My girls know it," Freddie replied.

"Do you want to pull out?"

"Let's stop talking, you're too fat to waste your wind."

"Am I?" yelped Kate and swung a right.

The fist caught Freddie's cheek and staggered the girl, but she caught her balance and bored in as Kate rushed her. Ramming her left hand into Kate's belly, Freddie chopped a right to the blonde's cheek and clipped her again with the left. For five minutes, while their girls yelled encouragement, Freddie and Kate fought with their fists like two men. It became apparent that Kate took the worst of the exchange. Although her blows landed heavier, Freddie got in three to Kate's two. Twice she put Kate down, but hit the floor herself when a good, solid blow landed.

Jumping forward, Kate raised her foot. Freddie had started one of Kate's eyes swelling up and blood trickled from the blonde's nose. Pain and anger made Kate start the rough-house tactics. However, before her foot could crash down on to Freddie, the brunette caught her other ankle and brought her down. Then Freddie made an error in tactics. Flinging herself on to Kate, Freddie found that she had caught a tiger by the tail. In a close-quarters, roll around brawl, Kate had the advantage of weight and experience. Not that this showed at first for they twisted and rolled over and over on the floor, scattering their girls before them, throwing wild slaps, punches and bites at each other, entwining their legs or flailing them wildly. First one then the other would gain the upper position, raining blows on the underdog until violent heaving and pitching threw her off and put her underneath. However, Freddie found herself being harder and harder pressed to turn the heavier girl.

With a heave, Kate twisted Freddie from her and threw a fat leg over the other girl's body, sitting on Freddie's stomach and grabbing at her hair. Although Freddie tried, she could not turn Kate over. Her struggles did prevent Kate from taking advantage of the upper position, but it was only a matter of time before the weight licked her. Desperately Freddie swung her fists up at Kate and made the blonde lean back to avoid the blows. Then Freddie brought up both her knees, driving them into the blonde's back. Even this might have failed to move Kate, only Freddie had a bit of good luck.

At first the girls obeyed their bosses' orders and kept apart, but the ebb and flow of the fight round the room had caused them to mingle and join in a circle. Tension rose higher with the excitement as the girls screamed encouragement to their respective bosses.

Among the girls, Babsy buckled down to a top-class job of encouraging Freddie with her usual gusto. Then somebody bumped into her hard enough to make her turn and look who it was. Of course it had to be Ginger. Recognition was mutual and the reaction immediate. Four hands shot into hair and the two girls spun around, struggling with each other, crashing into Kate

just as Freddie rocked her off balance. The impact
threw Kate from Freddie and, as if triggered off by
Babsy and Ginger, everybody in the room started
fighting with her neighbor, in some cases without
seeing, or caring, that she tangled with a friend and
fellow-worker.

Feet kicked and trampled over Freddie before she
could force herself upright. Shoving a couple of
struggling girls aside, she threw herself at Kate just as
the big blonde rose to her feet. With hands locked into
hair, they reeled back and Freddie smashed Kate into
the bar with enough power to wind the blonde. It was
now Freddie's advantage. Releasing the blonde hair, she
whipped two slaps then a punch across Kate's face,
rocking her head from side to side. Then Kate had some
luck for a swarm of screaming, fighting girls descended
on them and forced them apart. Freddie spent the next
couple of minutes fighting her way clear of the girls but
the moment she and Kate met again, they found more
girls impeding their business.

A screeching girl leapt on to Freddie's back and two
more tangled with Kate. Reaching over her shoulder,
Freddie grabbed her attacker's hair, bent double and
shot the girl forward on to the floor. At the same
moment Kate managed to grab her two assailants by the
necks and crack their heads together. Dropping the limp
girls, Kate looked at Freddie.

"This's no good!" Freddie gasped, knocking aside
another girl. "Let's go into my office!"

"Sure!" Kate gasped.

They fought their way across the room with an effort
and entered Freddie's private downstairs office. To
prevent further interferences Freddie locked the door. It
seemed that she anticipated using the office for this purpose, for all its furniture but the big desk, which had
been shoved back against one wall, and the safe had
been removed.

"How about a drink before we start again?" Freddie

asked, wiping blood from the side of her mouth. "There'll be nothing extra in this one."

"I found out what happened," Kate replied leaning against the wall and sniffing through a nose which felt twice its normal size. "Damned fools."

"Did they do much damage in the fight?" Freddie inquired, taking a bottle of brandy and two glasses from the desk cupboard.

"I've hardly a whole chair or table left."

"Can you afford to replace them?"

"No. I paid out all I had to buy the Buffalo in town. Things had been as slack in Brownton as down here and my overheads ate away my savings."

"Look," Freddie said, handing Kate a drink. "I feel responsible—"

"Don't offer me charity" Kate warned.

"Sip that brandy and shut up," Freddie answered. "I'm not thinking of offering charity. I think you and I could make a good team. I have some capital and you have experience. Let's be partners."

Kate gagged as the brandy went down the wrong way in her surprise. She stared at Freddie for a moment and gasped, "Are you serious?"

"My father always told me to be serious when discussing money. Is it a deal, old girl?"

"You've got a partner," Kate grinned and held out her hand.

"We'll have the lawyer tie it up in the morning, or whenever we can get out of bed," Freddie said, shaking hands with Kate.

"Huh?"

"Just because we're partners doesn't mean our little party's over," Freddie explained. "I can't bear suspense and we'll both want to know who is boss."

"You know something," grinned Kate. "You're right at that. Put the glasses away, junior partner, and let's away to the ball."

After Freddie had locked away the glassware, she and

Kate circled each other, then closed and the fight resumed with as much ferocity as they had shown when still rivals.

In the barroom an equally hectic and wild battle raged. It may have started as Fair Lady against Buffalo, but now nobody cared who she fought with as long as she fought. It became a matter of kick, punch, slap, scratch at, bite on and tear hair from the nearest body regardless of who the body worked for.

Only Babsy and Ginger managed to stick together and it went hard for anybody who tried to come between them. Both girls gave out with a considerable amount of energy for they always threw themselves whole-heartedly into anything they found themselves doing. All went reasonably well until Ginger ripped the shoulder strap of Babsy's dress and tore the material down the side. Staggering back a couple of paces, Babsy screeched like a scalded cat. One look at Babsy's face set Ginger flying for safety behind the bar. Babsy followed her and tackled her. Kneeling on Ginger's body, Babsy gripped the redhead's dress and tore at it until she ripped it off. With a howl of rage, Ginger threw Babsy off and dived at her, hands grabbing cloth. Neither would be seen again for some time but notice of their presence showed in screams, scuffling sounds, ripping noises and the occasional piece of a garment which flew up into the air.

Freddie and Kate fought on, ignoring the lessening sounds of strife from the barroom. First one then the other appeared to be on the verge of victory during the wild thirty minutes they fought in the office. Each time the apparent loser would manage to rally just in time and fight on. They fought with their fists like two men, showing a fair knowledge of wrestling in throws and holds, using women's tactics in their struggle for mastery. At last both were on their last legs and the barroom had been silent for some minutes. Both were naked to the waist and mottled with bruises as well as sporting four blackened, swollen eyes between them, bloody noses and puffed-up lips. Their hair resembled twin dirty mop heads and a fair amount lay scattered around the room. Freddie's tights had no knees and the right leg no longer had a foot, while Kate's jeans left leg flapped open along its seams.

A shove from Freddie sent Kate down on to her back and as Freddie dropped on to the blonde, two plump, powerful legs locked around her waist. The pain was intense and Freddie fought to free herself. More by accident than design she managed to rise, although with the legs still around her. Sliding her arms under Kate's legs, with the blonde hanging down to the floor before her, Freddie fell backwards. With her knees against Kate's back, Freddie used their leverage to lift the blonde's torso from the floor. Kate came erect and fell forward, her head striking the wall. Instantly everything went black and Kate collapsed in a limp heap on top of Freddie. Not for a few seconds could Freddie wriggle from under the plump body. Sitting up with Kate crumpled on her knees, Freddie reached out a hand meaning to pull the blonde into a sitting position and deliver a *coup de grâce*. The effort proved too much for Freddie and she slumped forward over Kate's limp frame.

"Sure quiet in there," Lily Gouch remarked, looking across the street.

"Let's go pick up the pieces," Big Sarah replied.

Quite a sight greeted them as Sarah unlocked the doors. One thing was for sure, neither saloon could claim a definite, or even possible, victory. Tables had been overturned, chairs broken or thrown aside, odd items of clothing lay or hung around the room; but not one girl remained on her feet. They lay in piles, pairs, singly and every one of them sported marks of the fight.

"Go get your gals, Lily," Sarah said. "This'll've cleared the air a mite."

As there still appeared to be activity in the private office, Sarah went around the girls to see if any might be seriously injured. Apart from scratches, bites, bruises and a little minor blood, there appeared to be nothing to worry her. Missing Babsy and Ginger, Sarah searched for them and found them behind the bar. Both girls always boasted they never did anything by halves and so it seemed. They lay side by side, bruised, battered and as naked as the day they were born.

Chuckling, Sarah crossed the room to the office. After a louder than usual crash it had gone silent. When she unlocked and opened the door, she found Kate and Freddie piled on the floor.

"Oh no!" Sarah groaned. "If it's a draw we'll have this lot again as soon as they're well."

CHAPTER FIFTEEN

Showdown in Brownton

Kady Jones was an honest man. Although he once hired out his gun, it had always been understood that he faced down only men who could defend themselves. Never did he cross the thin dividing line between what the West classed as killing and counted as being murder.

From what Jones heard while standing at the deserted bar of the late Lefarge's saloon, he reckoned it to be time he pulled up stakes and parted company with Marshal Banks Fagan. Many things Jones had learned and seen about Fagan chilled him and drove out any liking or respect he might have felt for the man. However Jones always remained loyal when hired and he overlooked the marshal's failings. Incidentally this was the reason, Jones' loyalty, that made Fagan hire him; the marshal feared that one day some enemy might employ Jones to take revenge and so made sure the situation did not arise. Jones had given Fagan good service, but drew the line at becoming an accessory to a crime. While he might be a killer, Jones had never been a thief.

A sardonic grin creased the gaunt deputy's ugly face as he watched Mayor Grief nervously pacing the room, Fagan sitting at a table and drinking Lefarge's whisky and Buxton, the man employed to spy on Mulrooney, leaning against the left side window, looking along the trail to Mulrooney. They acted about as scared and jumpy as a bunch of whitetail deer in the heart of hotly-hunted country.

"Is there any sign of Crocker, Buxton?" asked Grief for the tenth time in thirty minutes.

"No."

"You don't reckon he's double-crossing us, Banks, do you?"

"Who, *Vince*?" asked Jones sardonically.

"He's not double-crossing us. Those boys with him wouldn't give him a chance and their only way of getting clear of Kansas is with my help," Fagan replied. "I don't make mist—"

"Hell fire!" Buxton croaked, staring bug-eyed out of the window. "It's him!"

"Who?" asked Fagan, sticking a cigar into the corner of his mouth.

"Dusty Fog!"

The cigar fell from Fagan's mouth and Grief stopped his pacing, staring at the marshal.

"It went bust!" Grief croaked.

"If they took Crocker alive, he'll be talking up a storm," Fagan growled, showing a shrewd judgment of his man's character. "Is Fog alone?"

"There's no sign of any of his bunch with him," Buxton answered after taking a further look along the street.

"That figgers," the marshal grunted. "Fog's a cowhand, not a lawman and he's the sort to make a grandstand play."

"What'll we do? asked Buxton, glancing at the back door of the room and showing all the ferocious eagerness to fight of a cotton tail rabbit seated by its hole.

"I know nothing of this affair," Grief stated. "I'll be le—"

"Stay put, Grief!" Fagan spat out. "You're in this as deep as I am. Make a move out of here and I'll put the whole blame on you."

The threat might have carried less weight if Grief did

not feel certain that Fagan would shoot him down on the spot should he attempt to leave. Running his tongue tip over fat, suddenly dry lips, he looked at the marshal.

"Wh – what do we do?" Grief croaked.

"Buxton, get hid behind the bar, there's a sawed-off ten-gauge under it. Grief, go into the office and cover Fog from there. You got a gun?"

"N – no."

"Get the other scatter from under the bar. Move!"

When Fagan's voice took on that wolf-savage snarl, folk who knew him watched their step – and both Buxton and Grief knew Fagan very well. Neither argued about his duties but headed for the bar, collected the shotguns and took up the positions as he ordered.

Hooves thudded outside, sounding loud in the Sunday afternoon silence. Fagan looked at Jones and there was sweat on his brow as he said, "We'll take him as he comes through the door."

"Not me," Jones replied. "I just quit."

"You what?" Fagan snarled.

"Quit. Q-u-i-t's how they spell it, means we're finished, Banks. I don't like being took for granted; I don't like the idea of a robbery that could ruin a bunch of decent folks. Comes to a real fine point, I reckon I don't like you. See you, Banks – maybe."

The hooves came to a halt outside and leather creaked as the unseen rider swung from his saddle.

"You can't run out on me, Jones!" Fagan spat out.

"So long, Banks," the ugly gunman replied calmly. "I'd like to say it's been nice knowing you; but it ain't, so I can't."

With that he made a bad mistake. Turning, he walked across the room, meaning to leave by the back door. Fury seethed inside Fagan as he watched Jones walk away. Fury and fear mixed. Outside the saloon Dusty Fog was coming; the fastest gun in Texas was headed into the barroom to arrest Fagan and now Jones had quit cold, left the hand that fed him at a time when

Fagan needed help most. Dropping his hand, Fagan drew his gun and lined it at Jones' back. Too late Jones tried to turn as he heard the sound of a cocking Colt behind him and guessed what must be happening. Fagan's gun roared, kicking against his palm and sending lead into Jones' back as the gunman twisted around, hand fanging to the butt of his Army Colt.

And then all hell tore loose in the saloon.

Dusty tore through the batwing doors, coming with his matched Colts in his hands. Quickly his eyes took in the scene before him. Fagan standing with a smoking gun after cutting Jones down, but starting to swing back towards the front doors. Worse still, the double barrels of a sawed-off ten-gauge showed through the slit of the open office door.

It was a moment of decision, with Dusty's life hanging in the balance and on the quickness of his re-actions. He decided the shotgun-user would be the more pressing danger and must be taken out of the game first. Left, right, left, right, the twin Colts bellowed out, throwing their lead at the office door with unerring accuracy. The shotgun's barrels tilted upwards, the right side tube discharging its load, but the buckshot went over Dusty's head. By that time Fagan had almost com-pleted his turn and was even then swinging his gun towards Dusty.

Crashes sounded as the left, rear and side doors of the barroom burst open to give admittance to Waco, the Kid and Frank Derringer. All saw the danger to Dusty and acted with speed.

"Fagan!" the Kid roared, levering off shots so fast that his right hand looked no more than a blur and the empty cartridge cases curved into the air like they were being tossed out by a Gatling gun's ejector.

Throwing up the shotgun he had brought along, Waco cut loose on the marshal without any waste of words, emptying both barrels into Fagan and the eighteen buckshot balls did not have time to spread far when they struck flesh. Also armed with a ten-gauge from the Mulrooney's office's rack, Derringer triggered off both barrels in a rapid right, left, and he did not miss.

One way or another Marshal Banks Fagan, late of the Dakota Territory, was a tolerable dead *hombre* by the time Dusty's three deputies finished with him.

Rolling on to his stomach, Jones gritted his teeth and fanned off six shots from his already drawn Army Colt, sending the bullets into the front of the bar. Fanning had never been a target-accuracy method of shooting; but the gods of chance must have figured they owed Jones a break after his lapse from grace. His fifth shot sliced through the woodwork and into Buxton just as the spy started to rise and cut in – Buxton being under the impression that it had been Grief's shotgun he heard and so it called on him to show willing. Taken by surprise, Buxton reared upwards still holding the shotgun. Dusty saw the man and turned, his right hand Colt bellowing and planting a bullet between Buxton's eyes.

"Hit the office, Waco!" Dusty barked, leaping to Jones' side.

"Damned fool!" groaned Jones, watching Waco hold the shotgun in his left hand, draw his right side Colt and go through the office door with the smooth efficiency of a trained lawman.

"Me?" asked Dusty, holstering his Colts.

"Naw, *Me!*" Jones spat out the two words in a disgusted manner. "I should ought to have known better'n show Banks Fagan my back like that."

"What happened?"

"I'm no thief. Didn't know about that try at your bank until this morning. Then I figgered to pull out. Should've knowed Banks wouldn't go for that."

"Lie easy, I'll get the doctor over here," Dusty said and looked to where Waco shoved a scared and slightly wounded Mayor Grief from the office. This did not surprise Dusty, nor did the fact that he had only slightly wounded the man; he had been pumping lead out to distract the shotgun-user and hoped to make some of it count at the same time.

"Saw the young'n there ride through town a piece back," Jones gritted. "Only he wasn't sporting that badge then. And Banks allowed you wasn't a lawman."

Fagan's misjudging of Dusty's character had been the last mistake in a long mis-spent career.

On reaching the rim overlooking Brownton, Dusty took precautions. Keeping out of sight, he sent Waco into town to reconnoitre. The youngster did his work well, returning with word that Fagan and the mayor were in the Buffalo Saloon. So Dusty laid his plans accordingly. He sent his three deputies to make their way into town from the rear and surround the building. Giving them time to take their places, he then rode openly down the main street and held the attention of the men in the saloon. Waco had seen the lookout and reported on his presence, enabling Dusty to plan with more accuracy.

The success of Dusty's planning showed in the fact that he walked into a gun trap, but came out of it alive. Like Dusty always said, the lawman who used his head for thinking instead of butting wound up by living longer.

Although a hostile crowd of Brownton citizens arrived to investigate the shooting, Mayor Grief sent them about their business. He did not do this out of the goodness of his heart, but because the Ysabel Kid's bowie knife point pricked his back just over the kidneys and he had the Kid's solemn promise that failure to remove the crowd would be painful in the extreme.

"And that was the end of it," Dusty Fog told Freddie Woods that evening.

They were in Freddie's bedroom, which did not hint at romance. Even if Dusty felt romantically inclined, Freddie's battered face might have put him off; and anyway Freddie did not feel any desire to do more than lie on her back in the hope of easing her bruised and aching body.

"What about Jones?" she asked, having heard the full story.

"I had him brought here. He's not badly hurt and Kail Beauregard'll need a good deputy or two when he arrives."

"I'll see Jones is appointed," Freddie promised.

"Who won?" Dusty asked with a grin.

"I did – I think. Anyhow, *Kate* thinks I did and I'm not going to argue with my *junior* partner."

"Brownton's done. Most of its folks are pulling out," Dusty told Freddie. "I don't reckon there'll be any more trouble from that area."

"Or from this, now Kate and I are friends," Freddie replied. "Mulrooney has a lot to thank you for, Dusty."

"Forget it," Dusty replied. "Just see that it stays one town where a Texas man gets a square deal and I'll be satisfied."

"That I'll promise you," Freddie Woods replied.

And she kept her promise. Mulrooney received the spur line and grew. But no matter how large it grew, the town remained the one place in Kansas where a Texas man could go and know he would be treated fairly; thanks to those trouble-busters from the Rio Hondo, the men they called Ole Devil Hardin's floating outfit.

More shoot-'em-up action from

J.T. EDSON